P9-DZM-512

"You're so damned beautiful."

Holt drew back a step. "We shouldn't do this."

"I disagree," Cecelia insisted.

Of course she would. But it was a mistake, more on her part than his.

"I don't want to be gentle with you." He wanted to scare her, wanted to back her off. But it wasn't fear he saw in her eyes, it was...anticipation.

"So don't be gentle." She tugged at his tie and slid it out of his collar.

"Cecelia." It was the only coherent word he could get past his lips.

"I'm right here."

Her fingernails scraped lightly across his chest.

"I'm not that white knight you're looking for," he said with an ache that almost undid him.

"I don't care."

WOULD-BE CHRISTMAS WEDDING

USA TODAY Bestselling Author

DEBRA WEBB

If you purchased this book without a cover you should be aware that this book is stolen property. It was reported as "unsold and destroyed" to the publisher, and neither the author nor the publisher has received any payment for this "stripped book."

Recycling programs
for this product may
not exist in your area.

ISBN-13: 978-0-373-74777-1

WOULD-BE CHRISTMAS WEDDING

Copyright © 2013 by Debra Webb

All rights reserved. Except for use in any review, the reproduction or utilization of this work in whole or in part in any form by any electronic, mechanical or other means, now known or hereafter invented, including xerography, photocopying and recording, or in any information storage or retrieval system, is forbidden without the written permission of the publisher, Harlequin Enterprises Limited, 225 Duncan Mill Road, Don Mills, Ontario M3B 3K9, Canada.

This is a work of fiction. Names, characters, places and incidents are either the product of the author's imagination or are used fictitiously, and any resemblance to actual persons, living or dead, business establishments, events or locales is entirely coincidental.

This edition published by arrangement with Harlequin Books S.A.

For questions and comments about the quality of this book, please contact us at CustomerService@Harlequin.com.

® and TM are trademarks of Harlequin Enterprises Limited or its corporate affiliates. Trademarks indicated with ® are registered in the United States Patent and Trademark Office, the Canadian Trade Marks Office and in other countries.

Printed in U.S.A.

www.Harlequin.com

ABOUT THE AUTHOR

Debra Webb wrote her first story at age nine and her first romance at thirteen. It wasn't until she spent three years working for the military behind the Iron Curtain and within the confining political walls of Berlin, Germany, that she realized her true calling. A five-year stint with NASA on the space-shuttle program reinforced her love of the endless possibilities within her grasp as a storyteller. A collision course between suspense and romance was set. Debra has been writing romance, suspense and action-packed romance thrillers since. Visit her at www.debrawebb.com or write to her at P.O. Box 4889, Huntsville, AL 35815.

Books by Debra Webb

CAST OF CHARACTERS

Emmett Holt—Deputy director of Mission Recovery. Holt took Lucas Camp's place when the older man retired. Some believe Emmett will do anything to move to the top, but will he stoop to using Director Casey's sister?

Cecelia Manning—Thomas Casey's sister, widowed over a year ago. Before making the career move from CIA administration to operations, she's planned to throw a charity gala in memory of her husband—but a new love interest might interrupt her plans.

Thomas Casey—Director of Mission Recovery. Thomas is the consummate specialist. But someone is determined to take him down and expose Mission Recovery.

Casey Manning—CIA agent, Cecelia's daughter and Thomas Casey's niece. She's newly married to Colby investigator Levi Stark, and visiting Alexandria to support her mother's charity gala.

Bernard Isely—An international criminal who will stop at nothing to have his revenge on Thomas Casey and Mission Recovery.

Lucas Camp—Thomas's closest friend and Casey's godfather. He will do whatever necessary to protect his friend and Mission Recovery's secrets.

Victoria Colby-Camp—The semiretired head of the Colby Agency. She and Lucas can't seem to stay out of the business of investigations.

Chapter One

So this is how it feels to be a traitor.

Emmett Holt exited the metro at the Mall. Of all his less-than-admirable traits and accomplishments, this one had brought him to an all-new low.

There was no going back from this, no explanation or excuse he could offer for the damaging evidence he was about to hand over. While it was only a flash drive, it felt like a fifty-pound weight-lifting plate from the gym. He knew Director Thomas Casey had someone tailing him and he knew better than to waste time trying to make that identification.

If this sting backfired, if either Thomas Casey or his nemesis, Bernard Isely, got impatient, Holt—standing between them—would get cut down in the crossfire. Not exactly the way he'd seen himself going out of this business, much less this world.

Handing over the reports from the Germany mission when Casey had killed Isely's father was a stop-gap measure. Isely wanted both the intel on the old mission and the vial of the deadly virus Mission Recovery had seized two months ago.

It didn't take a genius to know Isely wanted a whole hell of a lot more than that. The man had one goal: to exact revenge and destroy Director Casey.

Holt was running out of excuses to keep both men at bay. And timing was everything.

He walked with purpose toward the National Air and Space Museum gift shop, just another man picking up another gift amid the throng of tourists. The weather was clear and the wind cold, but winter hadn't turned truly bitter yet and people were still wishing for an idyllic white Christmas.

Holt could only wish he would still be alive come Christmas.

He stopped where the text message had told him to stop, feeling like a damned puppet on a string. Even knowing at the beginning that it would come down to this didn't make it easier to stomach the reality of doing so. He was used to giving orders, not taking them.

Handing over this tiny piece of technology and

the huge intelligence it stored marked the beginning of the end.

It might have been a few years since his last field op, but the skills didn't go away. They were far too deeply engrained. He checked his phone, made the drop and didn't die or get arrested as he walked back to the metro station.

"Did my warning help?"

Holt didn't miss a step as Isely joined him on the escalator. "Sure."

After receiving a picture of Director Casey's sister, Cecelia Manning, and the single warning of "Beware," Holt had dug into the woman's recent history to see what threat or purpose she might pose for Isely. Or for him.

He'd learned all kinds of details he didn't want to know, from her favorite perfume to her tight circle of wealthy friends who toddled about doing charitable works.

Then he'd found the big splashy occasion he knew Isely had been looking for: the charity gala the widow had organized to benefit cancer research in memory of her late husband. The event offered the perfect opportunity.

"And?" Isely prompted.

Holt wasn't inclined to answer truthfully. He'd exhausted himself planting bugs in the woman's house, a GPS tracker on her car, opening a profile that matched hers on an online dating site and monitoring her general safety while maintaining his own responsibilities at Mission Recovery.

"And her family will join her at tomorrow's event," Holt replied, giving the man what he wanted.

"You will take the appropriate action?"

Holt nodded, letting his hand shake just a touch. He didn't want to oversell it, but a traitor would have reservations and a few jangling nerves at this point. He had a wild hope that a specialist would come charging in—now—before this got messy.

"I will send the address when it is time."

Holt nodded again as the train came into the station.

"Don't worry, my friend." Isely's hand landed heavy on Holt's shoulder. "You have a new team now. You are not alone."

Friend?

Isely couldn't know it, but that was Holt's worst fear.

Chapter Two

"I know you're disappointed, Mom."

Cecelia Manning filled two mugs of coffee and handed one to her daughter, Casey. She watched Casey add a scant teaspoon of sugar and a hefty dollop of milk.

When the risk of milk ending up on her counter was minimized, she said, "My application was accepted."

"What?" Casey's mouth dropped open in shock. "You can't be serious."

"I am completely serious," Cecelia replied. She decided hiding the pain her daughter's reaction had caused was best for now. Neither her daughter nor her brother approved of her desire to go into fieldwork for the CIA, but Cecelia had had more than she could take of the boredom and routine of pushing paper around the agency office.

Her husband had worked in the CIA for the

entirety of their married life, until he'd passed away just over a year ago.

Her brother was the director of an elite team of covert agents known only as "Specialists." Her daughter had gone into CIA fieldwork, as well. Yet they all expected her to…what? Continue in her predictable, safe role, making Sunday dinners and birthday cakes and learning to knit while she waited for Casey and her new husband, Levi, to provide the grandchildren she wanted to spoil.

She sipped her coffee and saved the scream of frustration for when she was alone again.

"Mom, you can't."

"Can't?"

Casey's eyes flared as she obviously caught the warning Cecelia had packed into that one word.

"I didn't mean *can't* like that."

Cecelia sipped her coffee, waiting. More than a little curious how her daughter intended to wrench her foot out of her mouth.

"It's just…" She shrugged. "You're my mom."

Cecelia traced the handle of her bright stoneware cup.

"Fieldwork is crazy," she added.

Holding her daughter's gaze, she waited for an intelligent argument to arise. Not that she'd let anything deter her from her plans. Since her husband's passing, she'd merely gone through the motions of day-to-day life and now she was ready for something new. She *needed* something new... Like a life where she felt needed and...wanted.

She'd survived the shock and grief of losing the man she'd loved and expected to grow old with. She'd learned to cope with a quiet house and the sympathetic looks of her friends and neighbors.

Her work had been an anchor, steadying her as she moved from one stage to the next. Now it felt like a stone dragging her to the bottom of the Potomac when she thought of sitting behind a desk for the rest of her working days.

With William buried and their daughter a happy newlywed, Cecelia's life, unexpectedly, was her own, and she was determined to see just what she could do with it.

"Mom? You're not even listening."

"No," Cecelia admitted. "I'm not. Whether you approve or not, I'm making this move."

"Mom."

"Casey." She mimicked her daughter's exasperated tone. "I appreciate your concern, but I didn't leap into this blindly. This decision isn't a whim or even a midlife crisis." She saw Casey blush and knew her daughter had indeed suggested those unflattering theories. She and her uncle, Cecelia's brother, had discussed this move at length. "The agency wouldn't have accepted my request if I didn't have the physical or mental fortitude to succeed."

She held up a finger. "If you dare mention the Equal Opportunity Act, I'll throttle you. Don't think I haven't learned a thing or two about minimizing risk already. I am not as naive or helpless as you seem to think."

Casey held up her hands in surrender. "You're a self-defense ninja."

"Don't you forget it, either." Cecelia smiled. "I know enough about the process to know my two closest relatives did not recommend me."

"That's not true."

Cecelia let the fib go unchallenged. Her family wanted the best for her, but they just had a different idea of what that looked like. "And don't worry. You've been through the training yourself. It's not like they're dumping me out on the street first thing Monday morning."

Casey sighed. "Wouldn't it just be easier to take some vacation and travel? Field operations isn't a game, Mom."

Her daughter's complete lack of confidence cut deep, but she supposed it was to be expected. When you walked one path for the duration of a relationship, changing directions was bound to stir things up.

Maybe there had been enough talk of change for the moment. "How is Levi?"

"He's fine. His plane gets in around eight."

"And being married is wonderful?"

"Yeah," Casey admitted with a secret little smile. One Cecelia remembered wearing long ago when she was that age. "You're sure you're okay with us spending Christmas with Levi's mom in Florida?"

"Of course. You're now part of his family, too. Don't worry about me. I have plans of my own."

"You do?"

"Sure. I bought a ticket for—"

The doorbell rang and Casey shot her a curious look. Cecelia only smiled as she set her coffee aside. "I have friends. We even do stuff," she added with a wink. "It's probably about tomorrow night."

Before she reached the front door, it opened and her brother, Thomas Casey, walked inside. The tension was a palpable force rolling off him and bouncing around the narrow foyer.

Worst-case scenarios bounded through her head before she regained control. She'd learned early in her role as a wife and mother that a cool head was the best asset she could bring to any situation.

"What is it?" She said a quick prayer that it wasn't his new wife, but her mind absolutely blanked when he laid his hands gently on her shoulders.

The doctor who'd explained William's terminal diagnosis had done that, wearing a similar grim expression and looking at her with an emotion caught somewhere between sympathy and pity.

She shrugged out from under her brother's touch and shook off the uncomfortable memory. Whatever had brought Thomas rushing into her home, she instinctively understood she wasn't going to enjoy the news.

"Casey's here," she said, stepping out of his reach. "Come on back to the kitchen and have some coffee."

"We need to talk."

She swallowed the bitter words dancing on the tip of her tongue. Why did her family have so little faith in her abilities? "Not if you're here about my move to ops next month."

"That got approved?"

She rolled her eyes. No amount of good manners could have stopped the exasperated reflex. Temper wasn't something she frequently indulged in, but right now she was ready to do the one thing she'd never done in her life: kick her family out of her home.

Casey brightened considerably when she spotted her uncle. After a warm hug, they stood side by side and faced Cecelia.

"Go ahead and say whatever you need to say." Let them try to deter her. Teaming up against her would get them nowhere. She was making the move to ops, regardless. She'd already made arrangements for a house sitter while she was training.

"Why don't you take a seat, Casey?" Thomas nudged her to the stool at the counter beside Cecelia. "You may as well know the truth of what we're up against."

"I beg your pardon?" Cecelia stared at her brother as a fresh wave of concern rolled over her. "What truth?"

"You have to go into protective custody. Today. Right now, Lia."

A chill raised the hairs at the back of her neck. Her brother didn't shorten her name unless he was seriously distressed.

"I'll go pack a bag for you, Mom." Casey hopped off the counter stool, but Cecelia stayed her with a look.

"Why do I need protective custody?"

Thomas slumped forward, leaning his forearms on the counter and lowering his voice. "The analysts picked up some chatter about you."

"Me?"

"You're in danger. A pawn in a bigger game," Thomas growled. "It's my fault." He pushed back from the counter and paced away, then swiveled back. "One of my enemies plans to kidnap you. At least that's the rumor making the rounds."

"Oh, that's going too far, Thomas. We both know none of your enemies could possibly know about me." Her brother was the director of Mission Recovery, a covert team so dark, not even the president was routinely briefed on their operations. When Thomas or his Specialists were in the field, their cover stories were solid, with no links to their real lives. The only way an enemy could know about his connection to her... Oh, dear God.

"He has a mole inside my team. The kidnapper is likely to be one of my own Specialists."

That was all Casey needed to hear. She slipped by Cecelia and rushed up the stairs.

"That's impossible. It doesn't make sense. Your team is devoted to you and their work. You hand-picked each one of them."

Thomas grimaced and scrubbed a hand across his short hair. "Well, I clearly made a mistake somewhere."

"Who?" Stunned, she took a moment to wrap her head around such a ridiculous idea. No one betrayed Thomas Casey. "Who on your team would dare to cross you?"

"It doesn't matter. I'm setting up an op to take him down."

Cecelia relaxed a fraction. "Then there's no reason for me to run and hide."

Thomas glared at her. Having grown up with him, she didn't find the expression so intimidating.

"Lia, this mole is devious. He's been operating right under my nose for months now. When we make the arrest, it's going to stick, but he's going to fight back. Locking down the evidence for this kind of thing takes time. I'm not going to allow you to get caught in the middle."

"Allow?" She laughed. "I'm a grown woman."

"I know that." He clasped her hands in his. "You're one of the strongest people I know."

"So we agree." She met the determination in his blue gaze with an equal measure of her own. "I'll be careful, keep your number on speed dial, but I'm not going into hiding, Thomas. Not under any circumstances. It's my turn to challenge myself."

Besides, even if she wasn't making this career change, she just didn't think she could manage that kind of drastic shift in her plans. Not in the middle of this holiday season.

Last year's holidays had been marred by her husband's death. She'd still been receiving sympathy cards amid the annual Christmas letters and greetings. The abundance of charitable donations made in his name had been kind and wonderful expressions from caring friends.

And nearly unbearable as she wrote out each and every thank-you note. She felt awful and it was as if every bright moment last year was eclipsed by the darkness of her loss. It had been sheer determination and more than a little detachment that had got her through.

Promise me you'll live your life. It was the last

coherent conversation she'd had with her husband before the aggressive brain tumor had made her a widow.

She'd been trying to honor that request, and she had no intention of letting a rogue agent and a vague threat get in the way. She was living her life.

"You can't be that selfish," Thomas barked. "Or that foolish."

She reeled back as if he'd struck her.

"I'm sorry. Sorry," he repeated, holding his hands up. "But don't you see if you're out there—" he flung a hand wide "—you become leverage they can use against me to get what they want?"

"For how long?"

"Pardon?"

"How long would you keep me in protective custody? Where would I be? What excuse would I give to the people who are counting on me this weekend?"

Thomas blinked rapidly and frowned as if he were trying to catch up. "I don't know. A couple of weeks, maybe longer."

That would never work. Cecelia shook her head adamantly. "This is the wrong time, Thomas. I realize you didn't plan this, but you know I have commitments."

"The charities and parties can manage without you."

"But I don't want them to. And I won't let a

vague 'maybe longer' interfere with my plans."
That was exactly what she was trying to change
in her life. The idea everyone else seemed to
have that nothing she did mattered enough that it
couldn't be cast aside at the drop of a hat.

"Cecelia, please cooperate. The man pulling
the strings on this won't hesitate to hurt you. He
turned one of my own people against me. He
nearly killed me a few times over between the
airport and Casey's wedding."

"And yet you made it." She patted his cheek.
He really didn't need to go so far in his effort to
talk her out of this move. "I'll make it, too—if
this threat to me even proves more than a rumor."

"I had years of field experience and another
trained agent at my side," Thomas protested.

"I'm not hiding."

"Mom," Casey hesitated in the kitchen doorway, a big suitcase behind her. "You might put
your friends in danger."

"That's hitting below the belt and it won't
work." Cecelia set her hands on her hips. "Your
father didn't marry a bubble brain, no matter how
the two of you believe otherwise."

"You're twisting things up," Casey said. "This
has nothing to do with your career change."

"Maybe it should." The words were out before
she'd really thought it through, but she warmed to
the idea immediately. "I'm taking leave through

the holiday until I report for ops training. Why not use me to trap the traitor on your team?"

"How can you help if you're a victim?" her brother demanded.

"If they make the attempt, you can close in and you'll have your rogue agent. If—big if—I get kidnapped, you'll have someone on the inside."

Thomas shook his head. "No way. I won't risk your life that way. Even if we wired you, this guy would either find it or jam the signal, rendering the exercise pointless."

Cecelia held her ground, undeterred. "You can get creative and use me as an asset, or stop wasting your breath. Even if you put me in a safe house, I wouldn't stay there." Not this year. She had plans, a ticket to the Caymans and maybe even a new friend who might be encouraged to join her on a holiday getaway. But she wasn't sharing that. As unsettled as these two were about her career change, she didn't want to see how they would come unglued over her personal secret.

"If you were asset material, I'd have recruited you already."

Casey gasped, but Cecelia gave her brother her most serene smile. "When is this kidnapping supposed to happen?"

"I don't have a hard date. The analysts are working on it."

"I see."

"Who is the mole?" Casey wanted to know.

"I've narrowed it down to two people."

Cecelia arched an eyebrow. He'd already avoided this question once.

"Has to be either my deputy director or his assistant. They're the only ones who have the access to the information we've discovered that has been leaked to my enemy."

"And your gut says who?" Cecelia pressed.

Thomas sighed, rubbed his temples. "My money's on Deputy Director Holt. He's the only one who would know where to start looking. I just don't think his assistant could manage this alone. As much as I hate to admit it, it has to be Holt."

Cecelia rode out the jolt of surprise, hoping the two people staring at her didn't notice. She thought about it for a minute or two as Thomas went on about how he was still having trouble accepting the man would turn like this. Cecelia sipped her coffee, found it had gone cold. She dumped it out and poured a fresh cup.

Okay, reality check. What were the odds that two men named Holt would come to her attention within weeks of each other, one working for her brother and another through the online dating site?

Didn't take a master spy to figure that out. Slim to none, she figured.

Might as well put it on the table. "Emmett Holt?" she asked.

"Yes." Thomas scowled. "How do you know his name?"

"A man by that name was a last-minute donor to tomorrow's gala fundraiser," she hedged. And he'd been flirting with her online for the past few weeks. Those emails and text messages had been fun and full of life, but those feelings were fading quickly with Thomas's bleak news.

She'd learned long ago that coincidences usually weren't a matter of chance. She wouldn't put it past her brother to encourage a member of his team to make a dating connection and set her up like this, just to keep an eye on her. And he'd be feeling pretty guilty if the man he assigned to such a task was working against him.

But Thomas didn't look the least bit guilty, only stunned.

She moistened her lips and asked the question. "You didn't know he contacted me?" If this wasn't Thomas's idea, she wasn't about to clarify the precise manner of contact had been a dating service. They'd balked enough at her career plans.

She held her breath, a big part of her hoping there really were two Emmett Holts.

"How does this guy spell his name?"

She glanced to her daughter. "Casey, bring me my purse, please."

"It's right here." Casey already had it balanced on the top of the suitcase.

"Aren't you efficient?" Cecelia pulled out her tablet and brought up the details about the charity gala she'd organized for the pediatric children's oncology unit in memory of William. "There." She highlighted the line on the screen that showed donor names, addresses and emails, and then turned it so her brother and daughter could see it. "I was told he called the office yesterday morning, asked how close we were to the goal and then donated the balance."

"Holt?" Thomas gaped at her.

"So it is the same man?"

Her brother nodded then growled. "Looks that way. Think about it, Lia, why pick your cause?"

"Generosity? Maybe he needed a tax write-off. That happens this time of year." She could tell her brother didn't put much stock in either possibility. Yesterday she'd thought it was the gesture of a wealthy man more than a little smitten with the gala's organizer. Now... Well, now he had more than a few questions to answer.

Just her luck. The first guy who managed to stir any feelings in her and he had an ulterior motive.

"This would put him right next to you tomorrow night."

"You're being melodramatic." Truth was she had asked for tomorrow's seating chart to be adjusted when she learned he would attend. She'd had every intention of getting "next to him" and thanking him personally during their first real date, scheduled for this evening. She wasn't about to mention those plans in front of her brother and daughter.

"He might not even show up." She wouldn't think twice about having him tossed out if he didn't clear up a few things tonight.

"Oh, he'll show." There was a calculating gleam in Thomas's eyes. "And he'll find a way to kidnap you. It's the perfect venue and it would be a terrible embarrassment to me if I'm not there to protect you."

"That's absurd. Tomorrow's venue is perfect for raising money for the charity. Besides, I'll be surrounded by the trained agents and retired spies who make up our extended family all night long."

"Then it's a scouting mission," Thomas argued. "I'm telling you, Holt doesn't do anything on a whim. Every mishap of the past two months points directly to his office. This is the beginning of the grand finale. I can feel it, Lia."

Casey gave a thoughtful hum. "Wouldn't a guy who's made it to the second in command at Mission Recovery be more careful than that? Sounds a little half-baked to me."

Cecelia could have hugged her daughter. She thought the same thing, but knew Thomas wouldn't have entertained the suggestion if she'd offered it. It wasn't that she blamed him—he only wanted to protect her—but she was weary of being overshadowed and underestimated.

As the wife of a CIA operative, she'd learned to support and assist her husband in the real world, she had her own security clearance and even though she'd spent her career to date in the completely safe admin side of the agency, she knew how to think through a problem like an operative.

Her daughter's and her brother's consistent underrating of her was her own fault, she supposed. She'd let it happen by design and circumstance. They were used to her in a certain role: sister, mother, head chef, cheerleader and most recently caregiver and occasional confidant. Change was difficult, and she hadn't discussed her plans with them; she'd just put in the request to move to ops.

She'd told herself it was to see how she fared on her own merits, but it was just as much about delaying their inevitable resistance.

"Relax, Thomas. I'm safe and I'm perfectly capable of staying that way." She infused confidence into her voice. "You'll both be at the event tomorrow and we'll be surrounded by a room full of people. Go vet the hotel security staff if it makes you feel better." She wrote down the contact name from her notes. "Your Mr. Holt can scout all he wants, but we all know he won't be able to lift a finger against me. At least not and get away with it."

Thomas took the note and stalked out of the house without another word.

Cecelia turned to Casey. "Well, since you've got everything packed, I might as well go check in at the hotel and make Thomas happy."

"I can move there with you. Keep you company."

Cecelia bit back the frustrated reply as she loaded the used coffee mugs into the dishwasher. "You stay here like we planned and enjoy some quiet with your new husband when he arrives." She'd have to put this place up for sale one day, but it didn't have to be today. The place was just too large for her to keep up on her own. Especially if she was away a lot.

"We came to see you, Mom."

"And I appreciate it, sweetheart. We both know your uncle's already assigned a detail to hover over my shoulder." She flicked a hand in the direction of the street. "I know for a fact the Millers haven't had a week's worth of plumbing trouble and yet the van is still out there."

Casey walked toward the front window to look. "He just wants to keep you safe," she said with a soft laugh.

"I know that. It's only a ten-minute drive to the Plaza." She was already mentally adjusting her plans to give her date a chance to explain himself before Thomas barged in and wrecked it.

Was she that desperate? Maybe.

Whatever Emmett's reasons for reaching out to her through the online dating site and making the donation, she felt there was potential for a *real* connection between them. What she didn't feel was that he posed any threat to her.

Thomas would call that naive. Casey would call it wishful thinking.

She called it intuition, and she'd learned to trust her instincts long ago.

Cecelia was going on that date.

Chapter Three

Emmett Holt braced his elbows on his knees and caught his breath while he unwound the hand wraps protecting his knuckles from the heavy bag. The sweat dripped from his brow, trickled down his arms. Most days a hard workout cleared his head, but he'd been balanced on the edge for too long.

He recognized the signs, knew the inherent danger, but there was no going back.

Not now. He glanced up at the news ticker scrolling across the bottom of the television screen. No inexplicable illness outbreaks. No one closing in on him here at the gym with weapons drawn and handcuffs ready.

Every hour that passed without incident only amped up his tension.

This game had very real, life-altering consequences. Life ending was more accurate. For the inevitable innocent victims, as well as Isely and his team of instigators who'd launched this frustrating drama.

He crossed the gym and locked his ankles into the inversion table, then eased back. For a long moment, he just let himself hang there, upside down, daring anyone to take a shot.

Neither side would make a move here, not in public. It was the shadows he had to worry about. And those were all around him...every move he made.

Hands fisted, he crossed them over his chest and started the first set of fifty crunches.

He focused on the count, only letting his mind wander once he was relaxed and stretching out the burn.

Isely still had the one thing Holt needed to secure: the last vial of a deadly new virus. And Holt had more of what Isely wanted: damaging information on Director Thomas Casey.

Years ago, Casey had gone undercover in Germany, disrupting an exchange that would have set the Isely crime family at the pinnacle of the black-market weapons business forever.

It was one of those rare, landscape-changing deals, and Mission Recovery had successfully stopped it.

That's what they did, the whole reason the team

existed. God, he was going to miss having that kind of clear purpose in his life.

Holt did a slow-burn second set, then paused to think some more.

He glanced around the gym, and though there were only a few other Specialists around, he felt like they were watching him too closely and with too much wariness lurking behind those neutral expressions. Did they expect him to just lose it with a violent outburst or remorseful confession? Which one of them had been on his tail when he made the drop for Isely?

Months ago he'd have chalked up the wide berth they gave him to being the deputy director. He wasn't popular with the team. That hadn't bothered him much before. His management style was simply different from Casey's, more aloof.

It wasn't his job to make friends.

But since he'd chosen to take this mission on his own, with no one else read into the situation, he felt the unavoidable onset of mild paranoia. Holt told himself to relax. Even if Casey had started to piece it together, he wouldn't have shared such a damning theory with the entire team.

Not yet, anyway.

Holt took a deep breath, reminding himself he'd been trained to succeed at all costs. It shouldn't be such a surprise that his current efforts made him a potential target. That's how he'd planned it.

He came back to an upright position slowly to avoid the disorienting head rush, then unlocked the ankle bar and moved to an empty weight bench to work on his back.

Everyone thought he was just a suit, sitting in the successor's chair. Days like this were a clear reminder to the team that his strengths went well beyond pushing paper and signing off on personnel evaluations.

"Sir?"

He recognized his assistant's voice, as well as her polished black pumps when Nadine stopped in front of him.

He sat upright and pushed a towel across his face. "What is it?"

"Two of the messages you've been expecting."

Holt tossed the towel over his shoulder and accepted the cell phone she handed him. One number was blocked, but the terse text message left no doubt the sender was Isely.

The clock is ticking.

Holt scrolled, switched to the voice mail message with a shake of his head. The world was full of ticking clocks.

The silky feminine voice, definitely a product of a private school, drifted into his ear and eased the tension in his shoulders. "Thank you for the substantial donation, Emmett. We've reserved a seat for you at tomorrow's event. We're thrilled that you'll be able to join us so we can personally express our appreciation for your generosity."

Cecelia. It was exactly the opening Isely had ordered him to create. He smiled, unable to temper his enthusiasm for their date tonight. He struggled to keep it in the appropriate perspective. She was part of the job, but he'd discovered a few layers under the polish that tweaked his curiosity.

After all, despite popular opinion, he was human.

Holt handed the phone back to Nadine. "Thank you."

She nodded. "Yes, sir."

"Do you have plans tonight?"

"No, sir."

He studied her, but couldn't be sure if she was lying. It didn't matter. They both knew she'd cancel her plans if necessary to fulfill his request. "I could use your help in Alexandria."

"Black tie?"

"No." So she'd seen his reservations for the weekend. The reservation he wanted her to see anyway. "A few hours of recon." Isely's impatience made him nervous. He wanted someone out there he knew he could count on. "I'll get you the details."

With a polite nod, Nadine left him to finish his workout.

He powered through the strength routine, Isely's ticking clock in the back of his mind as he hit the treadmill.

Specialist Blue Callahan, well, Drake now that she was married, stepped onto the machine next to him. Like the others, she'd been handpicked for her post within Mission Recovery and she'd met the man who'd become her husband on an assignment. She had, in fact, been backed up on that mission by none other than the one and only Lucas Camp.

There was no love lost between Holt and Lucas. The older man had a method and when Holt replaced him here at Mission Recovery, he'd developed his own methods. Holt had reason to believe that despite his retirement, Lucas had been poking around in Holt's professional life. Probably his personal life, too. It was never a good thing to have a man like Camp second-guessing decisions.

Lucas Camp was a master in the business of spying. But he was out to pasture now and he needed to get right with his place in the world of spooks.

Keeping his face in neutral, Holt's mind spun through the potential pitfalls and traps Blue's appearance might present to his timeline.

"Deputy Director," she said, acknowledging him with an easy smile. "Working hard?"

"Always." He increased the programmed interval workout to the next level. "Big plans for the holidays?" It seemed the question on everyone's lips this month.

"Not particularly. A party or two, then Noah and I are headed back to the island for a quiet celebration. You have plans?"

"About the same as last year." That was one detail the team knew for certain about him—he had no family and no inclination to create one.

The glance she slid him held a bit of concern. "If you're ever in the mood for a warm, quiet beach, you're welcome to stay in our guesthouse."

He nodded, unable to come up with a verbal response. Not because of the effort to maintain his pace on the treadmill but because she'd shocked him. No one on the team—other than Thomas Casey—had ever aimed a social invitation in his direction.

Blue looked for all the world like she meant it, but he knew her impeccable field skills and had to consider this approach might be a trap. "I'll let you know," he replied.

He got through the rest of his cardio without incident and headed toward the locker room to clean up. Half an hour later, as he walked upstairs in the direction of the solitude of his office, he had to forcibly turn his thoughts away from the likelihood that this might be his last hour in this building.

As Holt entered the suite of offices that included his, Specialist Jason Grant was waiting for him, kicked back with a magazine in one of Nadine's reception chairs. So much for solitude.

"Grant."

"Sir," he said, setting aside the magazine and getting to his feet. "Do you have a minute?"

Holt looked him up and down, recognized the relaxed demeanor of a man fresh from vacation—this time on a honeymoon. Grant was slated to replace him as deputy director when Holt advanced to the director's post. Assuming of course Holt didn't die or wind up in prison in the next week or so. "Marriage suits you."

"Thanks." Jason rocked back on his heels, pushed his hands into his pockets.

"Come on in." Holt left the door open as he entered his office, counting on Jason's choice to close it or leave it open to give him a clue about what might be on the younger man's mind.

The door closed with a soft click.

Holt took his seat, relieved there wasn't a weapon in his back or a bullet in his brain just yet. He needed just enough lead time to get through the next forty-eight hours.

Then he'd happily take whatever discipline Mission Recovery wanted to mete out.

He unbuttoned his suit coat and settled into his chair. Jason mirrored his movements, taking the chair across the wide desk.

"What can I do for you, Grant?"

"Just a quick follow up on the Las Vegas operation."

Anticipation pricked Holt. "That case is closed."

"I realize I failed you—"

"Relax." Holt tapped a pencil against the arm of his chair. "My evaluation doesn't read that way. As far as Mission Recovery is concerned, you did a fine job out there."

"But—"

"A piece of advice?"

Jason nodded.

"Let it go. There's nothing to clarify, nothing to be concerned about beyond the holidays and your next mission."

"Which is?"

Holt forced his lips into a smile. "To enjoy the holidays with your new wife."

But Jason's eyebrows were drawn together. "Permission to speak freely?"

Holt dipped his chin. "Of course." One day, if he didn't get caught in his own trap, they would need to be completely candid with one another as director and deputy director.

"I don't think I believe you."

Holt didn't move a muscle as more of that anticipation leeched into his veins.

"I've gone over it every way possible, sir," he added with more sarcasm than respect. "That whole business in Vegas felt like a setup."

"You have good instincts," Holt admitted. "And I agree with your assessment. If you're implying I had anything to do with it, I'd ask you to give that a great deal more thought before you say something you'll regret."

Jason's gaze narrowed, but he kept his mouth shut. Kudos to the young man. He was going to make a top-notch deputy director.

"I have nothing but respect for you and your talents." Might as well add a compliment to the ugly truth, Holt thought. He hesitated, could practically hear the figurative ice cracking under his feet as he prepared to share details better kept under wraps. "Ours is a world of secrets, as you know. We have a mole in Mission Recovery. You can only imagine the distress and effort we've put into making a solid identification, but the director and I are working to resolve the problem."

"How can I help?"

"You know Director Casey has a history with Isely. See what your Interpol connections can give us on his operations over there."

"Anything in particular?"

Holt gave in and sighed. Another lie was hardly going to matter at this point. "I want to pin down the biologist who manufactured this virus Isely has been trying to unload."

"You think Isely means to manufacture more?"

"It would be one hell of a residual income. Just see what you can turn up." Holt could only hope the diversion would keep Jason distracted until this God-forsaken mission was over.

When Jason left, Holt addressed the blinking icon that indicated he had another message on his cell. Blocked number.

They know. I have adjusted the timeline accordingly.

No! Holt's temper nearly boiled over. If Isely used someone else to kidnap Cecelia Manning, Holt would be forced to expose himself to one side or the other before he had the evidence in hand to clear his name and maintain Mission Recovery's anonymity.

It was impossible. No one here could possibly know. Not yet. Of course Director Casey would have suspicions. He was supposed to have suspicions. Holt had been feeding Isely information very few people could access. But he'd put the breadcrumbs in the system, left enough room for doubt so he could finish the task the right way without jeopardizing too much or laying Mission Recovery bare for the government vultures and rabid media to pick over.

Isely didn't have the franchise on making adjustments. Holt knew how to scramble, scrap and fight dirty when it was necessary. A few years behind a desk didn't change the core of a man.

For nearly a year now, he'd let Isely see what he wanted to see, a disgruntled, ambitious second-in-command who resented Casey almost as much as Isely himself. It had been the performance of his life and he wasn't about to abandon it now when he could almost see the end of these dark days.

Adjustment negates impact, he replied via text on the disposable and untraceable burner phone Isely had provided. Deep down, Holt knew Isely preferred the showy, public embarrassment that kidnapping Cecelia from the gala would provide.

Long minutes passed and Holt mentally composed and deleted at least ten incriminating text messages. If he sent any of them, if he left the director no room for doubt, it would make it damn near impossible to nail Isely before the bastard slipped away to run his operation from a non-extradition country.

Holt had put himself in so many different shoes and looked at this from everyone's perspective he'd almost lost sight of his own agenda. Protecting Thomas Casey was top priority and preventing the exposure of Mission Recovery was essential. He cringed to think of the careers ruined and lives irreparably disrupted if the worst happened.

Finally, the cell chirped with another text message. Proceed as planned.

He'd been close enough to Isely these past months that he knew his enemy believed this news would bring him relief. He'd portrayed himself to Isely as a man who needed the stability of guidance and a set schedule. But that was the act. Holt knew better than to trust Isely to keep the leash on whoever had been chosen to take over should Holt get caught or falter.

Isely had resources and he used them well. Holt was plan A. There would be a plan B eager to step up and prove their worth in order to gain promotion and prestige within Isely's operation.

Well, there was one sure way to keep Cecelia safe until Holt could move in on schedule. Holt crossed to his office safe, pulled out an alternate ID and a stack of cash and prepared for his date with the director's sister.

It was laughable. The stuff of comic tragedies. He was about to prevent a kidnapping by becoming a proper gentleman.

Chapter Four

Cecelia turned up the collar on her wool coat for the short walk to meet her friends at their favorite wine bar in Old Town. It was the place they'd brainstormed tomorrow's gala and it was fitting to celebrate their success with a toast there tonight. The temperature was dropping but the moon was bright overhead, and the crisp winter air cleared her head. She breathed deeply now, knowing in a few days' time she'd be breathing warm, humid air in the Caymans.

It was no surprise the dark sedan had followed her from the house to the Plaza hotel. When she thought about it, she realized one like it had either been parked at the corner of her block or shadowing her for the past couple of days. She walked on, resisting the urge to tell the driver to go back and report that Director Casey's sister could take care of herself. She should give Thomas some credit.

Clearly he suspected she'd balk at protective custody, and he'd brought the safety measures to her.

She was nearly to the bar when two men approached her. They wore U.S. Navy-issue wool peacoats over jeans and heavy boots, but that was where the resemblance ended. The hair broke regulation, as did the beards. Her first thought was they were longshoremen on leave, but Old Town Alexandria wasn't exactly a shipping hub.

"Ma'am?" They stopped just in front of her. "Excuse me. Do you know the area?" the taller man asked with a faint trace of a French accent.

Thomas's warning blasted through her and she told herself it was far too early in her budding ops career for paranoia. Her hands fisted around the car key in her pocket. There was security nearby in the dark sedan, and by now Casey and her new husband were probably watching from a rooftop, and Cecelia was close enough to the bar that she could call for help if necessary.

"Yes," she replied with a nod, determined to keep an open mind. "What are you trying to find?"

"Do you know the restaurant owned by the retired hockey player?"

She relaxed, releasing her grip on her key. They were French Canadian hockey fans. "Of course." She gave them directions and wished them a good evening as she entered the wine bar.

Looking around, she realized she was the first

to arrive, so she claimed a high-top table near the front window of the swanky little bar and waited for her friends. While she was thrilled with their progress and the news that they'd hit the pre-event fundraising goal, with every passing hour she was losing enthusiasm for the event itself.

Her daughter and brother would attend with their new spouses, and she'd be the lonely, courageous widow.

She rubbed at the fading indentation on her ring finger where her wedding band used to sit. Even after William's death, she'd worn it, not quite ready to part with it.

After Casey's wedding in October, she'd had it cleaned and stored it in the safe at the house. Her friends had been supportive and so far her family hadn't noticed. Or maybe they just hadn't known what to say. They'd probably been too distracted with news of her career change to notice a change in her jewelry.

Now here she was, intent on meeting a man who could be an enemy of her brother…of her. She was prepared. Cecelia might not carry a handgun in her bag, but she always carried her trusty Taser. She was far from an expert with handguns, but she'd taken the necessary classes for using the Taser.

"Cecelia?"

She swiveled toward the deep voice she recognized from a few phone calls. The polite smile she always wore in public slipped a little when she met the intense, gray-blue gaze of the man who'd approached her table.

Danger was her first thought, with *delicious* chasing right behind it. His picture on the dating profile hadn't been doctored. And it hadn't done him justice. Those eyes, so cool and clear, were framed by the stark contrast of slashing dark eyebrows, thick dark hair and chiseled features.

His mouth tilted up at one corner. "Emmett Holt." He extended a hand. "I hope I didn't startle you."

"Not at all, Mr. Holt." She struggled to remember to breathe. To remember her brother suspected him of a terrible betrayal. Instead, all his wit and charm in their previous online conversations danced through her mind. "A pleasure," she managed. *Please let him be one of the good guys.* It would be so unfair to wind up with a shark on her first dive back into the dating pool.

The upturned corner widened into a full-blown smile and his eyes crinkled a bit at the corners. She barely stifled an admiring sigh. "Forgive me," she said, searching for her composure. "Did I get the time wrong?"

According to her calendar, they were meeting at eight, after her toast with her friends. She had the sudden, bizarre urge to keep him all to herself.

Dating was going to be enough of a shock, but dating a man who looked like this? Tomorrow night would be soon enough to show him off. She felt flushed in a way she'd almost forgotten about.

"Not at all. I got to town early. Planned to have a drink to settle my nerves before you arrived." He leaned closer. "Dare I hope you're here for the same reason?"

She shook her head, feeling a goofy grin fighting for control of her face. "I'm meeting friends. A last-minute review for tomorrow's event."

"Ah." He looked around. "Smart planning."

"I tend to do that."

That half smile was back. "Just as you stated in your profile." He winked. "I'll just wait over there at the bar until it's my turn."

The way he said that launched a swarm of butterflies in her belly.

"Wait. Your generosity…" She trailed off, searching for words as a surge of unexpected emotion swamped her. "Well, we thank you."

"It's a good cause," he replied. "I'll be waiting at the bar."

She watched him walk away—drinking in the way his trousers fit his backside, like a woman too long stranded in the desert. Abruptly she realized he might catch her foolish behavior in the reflection of the mirror behind the bar.

She specifically made the effort not to check if

he'd caught her staring, instead turning her gaze back toward the door. Her willpower was rewarded as her friends came in together in a rush of cold air and happy voices. They raised a glass to success, double-checked every last-minute detail, right down to their personal shoe selections, and then parted company until tomorrow.

Half an hour had never seemed to drag more. Which was a terrible thing to be thinking. These were friends she had enjoyed for years. Friends who'd carried her through all stages of motherhood, a few lonely anniversaries and eventually her husband's diagnosis and decline.

Cecelia pushed all of that to the back of her mind. That was the past. Her future was waiting for her on the other side of the holiday season. And oh, my, her present was right there watching her from the end of the bar. With her purse and wool coat over her arm, she squeezed through the growing crowd to join Emmett Holt.

"Hi." Reminding herself she couldn't be certain about his motives and discovering her intuition was blurred by her shocking attraction to him, she didn't know how else to start. "Sorry to have kept you waiting."

"Not a problem," he said, offering her his seat. "I enjoyed the view. Would you like another glass of wine?"

"Just water, please." She didn't think alcohol

would help her manage her fascination and she needed to focus if she was going to get some straight answers out of him.

He signaled the bartender, and she had a tall glass of water with a wedge of lemon within seconds. The bartender leaned close. "How are things going, Cecelia?"

"Great. Thanks, Ted."

Ted glanced at Emmett and then back to her. "Do you and the ladies have everything all set for tomorrow night?"

"Definitely."

"Glad to hear it." He moved on down the bar to serve the next customer.

"A friend of yours?"

She glanced at Emmett while she sipped her water, letting the cool liquid soothe her dry throat. He looked a little perturbed with the bartender's familiarity. Was he jealous, or did he see a potential interference with his kidnapping plan? Her intuition couldn't pin it down. Granted, she hadn't tried dating since her husband died and she didn't know if this was business or pleasure yet—only that part of her was seriously hoping for the latter.

"My friends and I meet here almost every week," she explained. "You work in DC. Surely this isn't your first trip to Alexandria."

"No, it isn't."

Well, that was less than enlightening. She tried

a different tack. "Is there a particular area or way you'd like us to use your donation?"

He smiled, slowly, and though it was hard to tell in this light she thought maybe he blushed a bit. "No. You're free to use the money how you see fit."

"Okay." She watched him carefully, searching out any clues to his intention with her. But watching him carefully meant taking in the details. He oozed confidence and he obviously worked out. He was trim without being skinny and if his forearms were any indication, his biceps and shoulders would be beautifully sculpted.

He angled his body, effectively sheltering her from the crowded room and making this public encounter suddenly feel a lot more private.

Her heart rate fluttered, but with awareness rather than a more appropriate concern. He was close enough she recognized the citrus and cedar notes of his cologne. Her husband had preferred— she cut off the thought. That was *then*. This moment, this evening, was all that mattered right now.

Live your life.

But something else about Emmett reminded her of her husband and her brother. She'd been around the type long enough she would have picked up on it even without Thomas's warning this afternoon.

Emmett gave the appearance of being focused on her, but he was surreptitiously inventorying their surroundings and the people coming and going around them.

She'd caught her daughter doing the same thing more than once since Casey started working in ops. Situational awareness was a skill taught to field agents in the CIA as well as any other number of agencies. If she'd asked him, she knew he could give her an accurate description of everyone in the room and the best way out if any trouble cropped up.

He was definitely one of her brother's Specialists, and the last shred of hope she'd clung to that their meeting online had been a coincidence dwindled to zero. She needed a plan, needed to get to the bottom of his motives before she wound up used—or worse.

The man might have a generous streak, but it didn't require an active intuition to see there was more under the charming surface. "It was a pleasure to meet you, but maybe this isn't the best night for dinner. Let's talk more tomorrow at the gala." She slid off the stool just as someone behind him shifted, and she found herself pressed tight against his warm, hard body.

Speaking of situational awareness… She looked up at him, captivated by the cool gaze that only increased her body temperature.

"Why don't we go somewhere less crowded?"

Yes! "I'm not sure that's such a good idea." She inched away from him, fighting the overwhelming urge to get closer. "As generous as you are, we're scarcely more than strangers."

"I made a reservation for us at that steak house down the street."

The crowd shifted again, and this time he braced to keep from bumping into her. She was outrageously disappointed.

"Come on." He smiled and her heart jolted. "Let's share an appetizer and then you can decide if dinner is an option."

She felt herself nodding an agreement before she could voice a reasonable excuse.

He took her coat from her grasp and held it for her, straightening the collar and smoothing his hands over her shoulders. He retrieved his coat—a supple leather bomber-style jacket—from the hook just under the bar top.

He gestured for her to go first, and when she checked the reflection, she saw his eyes weren't on her, but the crowd around them. Something wasn't quite right. Was he protecting her or preparing to snatch her away?

Oh, she had to get her brother's voice out of her head so she could find her own way through this situation. She pushed through the door to the street and turned to just ask him outright, but another of his smiles completely derailed her train of thought.

"Is it always so crowded in there? It's a wine bar."

His beleaguered expression earned her sympathy. Apparently the profile notation that said he didn't like crowds was truthful. Giving him the benefit of the doubt, she said, "It's a popular wine bar. And every place is busier since we're closing in on Christmas." She gestured to indicate the white lights and holiday color dressing up the Old Town district of Alexandria.

"Fair point," he agreed, falling into step beside her.

"Was the holiday spirit what moved you to make that donation?"

His lips twitched and he ducked his head to avoid a low-hanging strand of white lights. "In part. I'm not typically one for the holiday spirit. Mostly it was you. After we met online, I poked around and found that video your organization posted. Who could resist?"

Plenty of people in this economy, she'd discovered. "What is it that you do, Mr. Holt?"

"You call me Emmett online," he reminded her.

His low voice sent a ripple of anticipation across her skin. "Emmett," she repeated, like a besotted schoolgirl.

"I'm in private security."

She turned her gaze toward the street, hiding her unjustified disappointment. Even if their on-line flirtation was genuine, she knew he wouldn't have told her what he really did and who he really worked for. It would have been a breach of security at this stage. Even as the director's sister, she wouldn't know Mission Recovery existed if she hadn't been married to a man like William. She told herself it was too soon to have any opinion on situations that fell into the delicate area of security clearances.

Still, she needed to know if he was here as friend or foe. "Ah, that explains it."

"Explains what?"

She shrugged. "The way you scout a room and keep track of people. Don't worry. It's not obvious to most women."

He gave her an arch look.

"I have relatives who are also in security-related jobs. Par for the course this close to DC," she added, wishing he'd take the bait and elaborate. Wishing she had the courage to demand clarification. It felt so uneven to be this attracted to a virtual stranger without any idea if his responses were sincere. It was an odd sensation to realize someday in the field someone would look at her and wonder the same thing.

"It's a habit we all develop, I suppose."

"A matter of survival," she agreed. "Or so they

tell me." Come January she'd be getting the train-ing firsthand. No more inferring from the vague references her family made. It was an exciting thought, and she grinned with anticipation.

"Now, that's quite a look, Mrs. Manning."

"Cecelia," she corrected. "I'm changing jobs after the holidays and whenever I think about it, I get excited."

"What type of change?" He pulled open the door of the restaurant and she stepped into the dim alcove.

"Just something more active." If he could hedge, so could she. It was good practice, anyway. "My company had openings in another department. All the recent charity endeavors made me realize I'm ready to get out from behind a desk."

He gave his name to the hostess and they were seated immediately. "What have you been doing?" he asked when they were settled in a cozy corner booth.

"I focus on basic administration for the human resources department. It's utterly boring, sifting through the same documents day in and day out. The job served its purpose while our daughter was growing up, but I'm ready to branch out now."

"You seem eager to try something new."

"Precisely." A man as perceptive as Emmett had probably already noticed that her hormones were willing to start that something new with him at the first opportunity.

The waiter came by with water and offered the evening's specials. They ordered drinks and the sampler of appetizers and Cecelia returned to her task of trying to unravel Emmett's motives.

"How long will you be in town?"

"Probably just through the weekend."

"Probably?" she echoed. Where had her conversational skills gone? He'd been trained to divert the curiosity she was so clearly showing, but she could do better.

"I'm really just here for you. For the gala," he added as though it was an afterthought. "Haven't had much cause to pull out the penguin suit lately, figured I should enjoy it. After that, it's back to work."

"In DC?"

"Same as everyone else in this area," he said with that half smile that made her want to sigh.

She agreed with a nod. "You won't take time off for the holidays?" Before her brother's announcement this afternoon, she'd been determined to boldly invite him to join her on a beach in the Caymans in a few days' time.

"Someone has to keep the office running. All the other guys have family." He shrugged. "I volunteer to stick around on holidays and put out the occasional fire so they don't have to."

"That's thoughtful of you."

One shoulder hitched in a casual shrug. "When you have kids, you should be there for them."

"That was my philosophy."

But now it was her turn to do something solely for herself… The problem was, this part may have been a mistake.

Chapter Five

Holt gave her credit for a gentle interrogation style, but he recognized the effort for what it was. It might only be first-date protocol, but maybe Isely had been right and Casey had started moving to intercept him already.

How to ask her what she knew without blowing it all to hell? That was the real question.

He started to ask then paused when the phone Isely had given him shivered in his pocket. It would likely be the address where he was supposed to stash Cecelia tomorrow night. He'd spotted a couple of Isely's men in the area already and the idea made him wary about being tailed.

"Excuse me one second."

He checked the phone and his stomach clutched when he read the terse message and recognized the address of a local warehouse. His worst fear confirmed. Isely's men had informed their boss that Holt and Cecelia were together and Isely wanted her tonight. *Damn it*. Holt needed to slow things down or his whole counter-operation would crash and burn. Isely might get a measure of revenge moving in on Cecelia tonight, but he wouldn't get the full effect Holt had promised when they'd been planning and negotiating terms.

"Problem?"

"No, not at all." He smiled and put the phone away. "Just a work thing."

"I understand. It happens."

She looked more disappointed than understanding. Her late husband had probably ruined many personal evenings with sensitive work distractions. Holt had the strange urge to show her a different side of men in security-related careers.

Not smart.

He turned the phone off and showed her the black screen before tucking it into his coat pocket. "There. I'm off the clock. Meant to do that earlier, but I needed the navigation app." Her smile was worth the lie. Worth all of the lies he'd been telling lately.

The appetizer sampler arrived and for a few minutes they just indulged in the cheese and cured meat selection. He couldn't remember the last time he'd felt this comfortable, this normal with a woman. Especially a woman who was a target.

Her manners were perfect society matron, but her little hum of appreciation as her lips closed over her fork had him thinking of other things.

Things he had no business thinking about with a woman like Cecelia Manning.

She was a gorgeous, walking temptation with her feminine curves, long golden hair and wide blue eyes. He knew from her profile and additional background searches she kept herself fit with tennis and yoga. Yoga meant flexibility.

A few images from the Kama Sutra zipped through his mind like a slideshow and he nearly choked on the cracker in his mouth. Giving in to lust wouldn't do either of them any good. If he lived through the next forty-eight hours, he might ask her for a do-over and take her on a real date that didn't involve looming thugs happy to do the bidding of a famous crime boss.

Of course, dating her for real meant Director Casey would definitely kill him. The entire concept was irrelevant. His career allowed no time for the sort of commitment a woman like her would require.

He caught her checking her watch. "Am I boring you already?"

"No, not at all." Her smile was apologetic. "Just a mother's habit. My daughter's new husband is flying in tonight. I'm expecting her to call or text and let me know he arrived."

"They came to support you for tomorrow's gala?"

"And an early Christmas weekend, just the three

of us." She sipped her wine. "They'll spend the real holiday with his mother in Florida. None of them are much for cold weather."

"What about you?"

"It doesn't bother me much. Winter's part of life." Her eyes went wide and she laughed. "I sound like some cheesy book on the self-help clearance rack."

"No apology necessary. Without winter we don't appreciate spring and summer. But a snowblower makes life easier."

"Very true."

"Is it a challenge?"

"What do you mean?"

"Watching your married daughter so recently after losing your husband?" He cursed himself. Hadn't meant to say that. Bringing up an ex was bad enough on a first date, but dredging up her dead husband, a man whom she'd loved deeply by all accounts? He was starting to understand why he didn't bother with dating. He sucked at it. "You really don't have to answer that."

"It's okay." She rested her fork against the small plate. "Losing William was the worst thing I've had to deal with." She took a deep breath and let it out slowly, worrying her lower lip with her teeth. "Well, you have some idea."

"Pardon?"

"You said you saw the video."

"Right. I did. Go on."

"Losing a spouse isn't an easy road, and getting past it doesn't seem to be something most people understand. This might sound harsh, but I can honestly say I'm comfortable with where I am now and who I want to become."

He couldn't reply. The emotions swirling in her eyes and that quick, nervous nip and release of her lower lip told him more than she wanted to reveal, he was sure. But her voice had been steady. She really was ready to move on with her life.

It made him feel even more like an ass for deceiving her.

The online dating thing had been the perfect ploy. The donation only added to the good-guy points he'd been racking up. By tomorrow, when she knew who he really was and why he'd approached her, she'd probably never forgive him.

Over the rim of her wineglass, she studied him, her expression contemplative.

To keep from squirming, he chose a successful field-tested tactic and went on the offensive. "Like what you see?"

"I think you know I do."

He leaned forward. "Want to do anything about it?"

"I believe I do." She leaned forward, as well. "Let's start with dinner."

They laughed, but there was no mistaking the

building sexual tension between them. The conversation continued as if they were old friends rather than potential new adversaries, until the meal was delivered by the manager, who took the opportunity to greet Cecelia and chat briefly about tomorrow's event.

When they had the table to themselves again, Holt glanced up from the task of slicing his steak. "Does everyone in town know you?"

"Only the people who've helped with the fundraisers. The manager here donated a romantic dinner package to the silent auction."

Holt took a bite and nearly sighed with pleasure. "I may have to make a bid," he said. "This is worth a second trip."

She grinned. "Good plan."

Things were going so well Holt almost let down his guard and enjoyed himself. What he'd started as basic recon after that nasty warning message from Isely had turned to a genuine long-distance attraction. He'd been captivated by the depth of personality she expressed in their emails and brief phone calls. She was much more than a beautiful widow with a caring nature balanced by brains and a clever wit.

In person, all of that was magnified. He was more than a little startled by how much he liked her. Typically, he didn't like getting to know people—so few were reliable and everyone wanted something—but Cecelia Manning was the exception that made him want to bend his rules about relationships.

Except this *wasn't* a relationship. He had to remember this was the most critical mission of his life. If he botched this, her hurt feelings would be the least of his problems. His boss would lose his sister and their covert team of Specialists would be exposed.

Holt had enough experience to know you didn't reach the goal by dwelling on all the things that could go wrong. There were already so many things wrong with this situation, starting with his general trepidation about ruining tomorrow's event, even by necessity. Yet dwelling on what could go right filled his head with thoughts of a more personal nature. If he'd suspected this kind of complication, he never would have opened an online dating account with which to lure her.

"I apologize," she said suddenly.

He questioned her with raised eyebrow.

"I've been rambling. I know you donated to the charity, but that doesn't mean you want to know about the minutiae involved behind the scenes. It's just filled all of my waking hours these last weeks."

"I enjoy listening to you." It might be the truest thing he'd said all night. Her smooth voice was like cool water after a long run on a hot summer day. It just rolled over him, easing the tension he'd been hauling around since his first contact with Isely.

"Uh-huh." She rolled her full lips between her teeth as if she was trying not to laugh. "You glazed over for a minute."

"If I glazed over, it was because I was thinking about things I shouldn't be thinking about."

"Work?"

"No." He loaded the word with enough meaning to imply he'd been thinking something much more personal and immediate. Intimate. And while it wasn't another outright lie, he needed to avoid all of the above. If he kept her out of Isely's clutches, she would never need to know the difference.

He reached across the table for her hand, then hesitated just before he touched her, giving her a chance to retreat. She didn't. Her gaze on his, she turned her hand over and used her thumb to trace the long scar that curved down the length of his index finger.

It was all he could do not to flinch from the gentle contact.

"Tell me about yourself."

"Not much to tell." He was a spy who didn't exist, a man who wouldn't exist if he didn't find a way to rein in Isely once and for all. He looked away, took in the perimeter of the room once more. "It was all in my profile. I'm not the sort to hold back."

She tipped her head to the side and traced that scar again. He wanted to tremble.

"I don't remember anything in your profile about this."

With her touching it, he was having trouble remembering the incident himself. The scar was a souvenir from a mission in Dubai. It had required minor surgery and months of rehabilitation for the nerves to recover and settle back to normal. If she kept caressing that thin white line, the nerves might never settle again.

"I slammed it in a car door and wound up needing minor surgery. Interesting process, really." He tilted his hand to look at it himself, but didn't withdraw from her touch.

"The recovery?"

"No. The surgery."

Her pale eyebrows arched and her whole body went still. He found himself fascinated by the reaction, wondering how she might react in other situations. "You watched them operate?"

"Sure," he said with a shrug. "They gave me a nerve block." Since he'd gone into the mission alone, he hadn't had anyone around to watch his back. General anesthesia would have left him too vulnerable.

"That's…"

Vulgar, sick, disgusting. He was ready for all of those words and worse.

"Amazing," she said, stroking her thumb across the ridge of his knuckles.

When had such a basic touch turned so damn hot? "Pardon me?"

"You heard me. Very few people have that kind of curiosity. Or courage."

"I don't know about courage." If he'd been wearing a tie, he would've tugged at it. Her eyes held something he'd rarely seen aimed his way—admiration. It left him speechless. He pulled his hand away. "Maybe I'm just an incurable insomniac."

She laughed, and he almost laughed with her, except one of Isely's crew chose that moment to lumber into the restaurant bar. The dark-haired man, whom Holt knew as Cal, took up residence on a bar stool where he could clearly observe Cecelia.

Isely's teams were nothing if not well trained. They were always in pairs, which meant at least one more man was waiting outside or in the kitchen, ready to take Cecelia off Holt's hands. Tonight was the wrong time to kidnap her, but Isely seemed determined to do so. What had accelerated his timetable?

Turning off the phone had clearly been a mistake. He should have anticipated the active response. Men like Isely, who were used to having every order obeyed out of blind fear if not devotion to the cause, didn't take it well when they were ignored.

"Dessert?"

"Not for me," she replied. "But I'll have a cup of coffee if you want to give the chocolate torte a try. It's marvelous."

He could tell she wanted to check her watch or her phone for word from her daughter. "I probably shouldn't keep you out so late," he said. "Your family is in town and tomorrow's a big day for you."

"Our walk-through this morning went well. Everything is in place and tomorrow is just a matter of the finishing touches." As if to emphasize the word, she touched him again. "I'm glad you'll be there."

"Me, too."

He hoped they would both be there. If Isely succeeded tonight, Holt's survival would be in the hands of the director. He didn't maintain much hope that that particular source of judgment would end in his favor.

"Let's take pity on the waiter and get out of here." He signaled for the check while she polished off the last bit of wine in her glass.

Times like this reminded him a lack of family was a good thing. Enduring a few lonely holidays was no real hardship if it meant there was no one to get hurt on his behalf. He knew these threats against Cecelia were harder on the director than any of the missions he sent Specialists out to salvage.

Business was one thing. Specialists were trained and willingly stepped into dangerous situations. But knowing an old mission and a current teammate had breached security to put a target on his sister's back? That would have any decent man twisted up and ready to shoot first and ask questions later.

It was one reason Director Casey's recent marriage baffled Holt. The man's personal philosophy of remaining a loner had been a solid foundation he'd adopted long before joining Mission Recovery. Covert operations just didn't mix well with family dinners, piano recitals and summer vacations. Even dating was a serious minefield when it got tangled up with the job.

"You look troubled," she said, pulling her hair from under the collar of her coat.

"Then it's my turn to beg forgiveness." He raised her hand to his lips and winked as he pressed a light kiss to her knuckles before she could put on her gloves. "Can I walk you back to your car?"

"You could walk me back to the hotel. I'm staying there through the weekend."

"You don't look all that happy about it."

"It was a last-minute decision. We moved gifts

and a few other things in today to make tomorrow easier."

There was more to it. His instincts warned he needed to know. "But?"

She opened her mouth to answer, but her phone interrupted them this time. Her smile when she checked the message led him to believe all was well with her daughter. Then it faded and she paled.

"Is something wrong?"

"Nothing serious."

He wasn't convinced, but he wasn't sure how hard to push. They were supposed to be new friends. "If there's something I can do, say the word."

"Thanks, but I'm sure it's just a mix-up." She shook her head, her blond hair swinging, but the smile on her lips didn't reach those stunning blue eyes. She tucked the phone into her pocket rather than her purse this time. "I'll just be glad when it all comes together tomorrow night."

"I'm sure everyone will have a great time."

She raised her crossed fingers. "And drink enough champagne to write big checks."

He laughed with her. "I left my checkbook at home."

She grinned up at him. "You've done enough already. My family and a few close friends bought tickets. It will be nice to see them."

Holt almost tripped. *Close friends?* Who could she mean? It would be bad enough kidnapping her out from under the combined noses of her brother and daughter.

"You aren't very convincing," he said, taking her hand in his as they walked along. It felt too right, too real. This was more than he'd bargained for and he was so much less than she deserved.

"Doesn't matter. I've chattered about myself enough for one night."

"Come on. I'm intrigued." He *needed* to know so he could be prepared. "Maybe we should make a plan so I can be a diversion." He wiggled his eyebrows.

"It's not a big deal." She gave his hand a squeeze. "They mean well and I know they love me. But no one seems very enthused about me getting on with my life."

"Because you're bringing a date to a charity event?"

"No." Her lips twisted in a wry grin. "Because they don't know I'm dating anyone seriously." Her eyes met his. "Tomorrow could get interesting."

He was sure of it. He'd carefully navigated the dating world so no woman would think to classify him as a serious prospect. He was the man women instinctively knew as the fun-while-it-lasted sort. It counted as a success that his efforts to woo Cecelia were convincing, but it unnerved him, as well.

He didn't want her to get hurt—by him or the ugly necessities of the op he was working out. Usually the mission was all that mattered to him. A hell of a time for *this* to happen.

Keeping an eye out for Isely's muscle, he felt the cold, calculating gazes of a surveillance team as they walked down King Street. His instincts were prickling, raising the hair at the back of his neck. Isely was obviously determined to take Cecelia as soon as possible.

Holt wondered at the rushed timeline and knew he'd have to get to a computer soon and see what he could dig up. Maybe Jason Grant's inquiries had set off some kind of alert on Isely's end of this dreadful business. The way things were going, it wouldn't surprise him to have inadvertently sabotaged himself.

In the reflection of a shop window, Holt recognized the man following them as one of Isely's personal bodyguards. The dark sedan that rolled by with government plates was probably a protection detail for Cecelia, courtesy of Director Casey. Just up the block, Holt spotted two more of Isely's men approaching.

Rock, meet hard place.

The dark wool jackets over jeans and heavy

boots made as much of a statement to an informed operative as a uniform with flashing name tags.

Holt knew Isely typically valued subtlety and he felt the unfamiliar twist of worry at this abrupt change in the man's method and instruction to his crew. Some new development had to be creating this urgency.

The man had been groomed to lead one of the primary black-market operations in Europe. Vengeance had its place, but even Bernard Isely had to know it paid to keep a cool head no matter the circumstances.

Swing music poured from speakers above a little club two doors down the street. He squeezed Cecelia's hand. "Want to dance?"

"Here?"

"Here could work." He did a quick twirl of their hands that brought her right up against him. She let out a soft gasp that lit a fire in his blood. The move put a sparkle in those big blue eyes and had the added benefit of suggesting both teams should take a step back. He brushed his cheek with hers to murmur in her ear, "But I was thinking in there would be better."

"Hmm. I could be persuaded."

"Good to know." Now they just had to cross the short distance without Isely's men doing anything stupid.

It was too much to hope for.

Isely employed them primarily for their willingness to follow orders without questions. If he'd hoped for the same blind cooperation from Holt, he was about to be disappointed. The bigger guy in the faded navy peacoat shouldered him—hard—as they passed. The contact was enough to jostle him against Cecelia and he had to reach out to keep her from bouncing into another couple on the street.

The guy had good hands, but Holt knew the burner phone had been lifted and replaced with a new one. What new intel had bothered Isely enough to take that kind of precaution?

Holt didn't have more time to think about it. The shorter man had grabbed Cecelia's purse and was tugging both the purse and the woman toward the narrow side street that cut through to the next block.

"Let go!" Holt shouted. He didn't care which one of them complied, but he sure as hell didn't want to get into a fight right here in the middle of King Street.

He heard the squeal of tires and imagined the director's surveillance team would be on them any moment. Cecelia shouted for the police and Holt noticed more than one onlooker pulling out a phone. To help or simply upload a mugging to the internet didn't really matter. He wasn't about to let this become a public spectacle.

He threw his body weight into the struggle and

drove both Cecelia and the would-be thief into the narrow side street and out of view.

The tall thug closed in behind him.

"Give us the woman," he growled, shoving Holt forward into Cecelia.

Accelerated timetable or not, Holt refused to hand over Cecelia to this pair. They were too rough around the edges and they looked too hungry. Had Isely put a bounty on her head? Spinning around, he raised his fist and drove a right hook into the tall man's ear.

The man staggered to the side, landing hard against the brick of the nearest building. The guy hadn't expected Holt to resist. Gave him a few seconds to rescue Cecelia.

But she was holding her own. He watched, stunned, as she used her strong grip on her purse straps to jerk her assailant closer and down, while she drove her knee up into his groin.

"Good girl," he said, coming to her side. He urged her toward the other end of the alley. If the squealing tires had been a team watching Cecelia, they weren't rushing in to help. He made a note to analyze it later. Right now they needed to escape. On the next street they could catch a cab and be safely out of reach in less than twenty minutes.

But the sound of glass breaking brought Holt back around.

The taller man wasn't giving up.

"Hand her over." He waved the bottle and charged, the sharp green edge coming closer, closer, until at the last moment, Holt blocked and turned. Determined, the taller man lurched back to his feet, advancing more cautiously this time.

Holt circled, keeping his face to the bottle-wielding thug and trying to get a line of sight on the other man. The shorter of their assailants squared up, flashing a knife.

Damn it. "Call nine-one-one," he barked at Cecelia. Drawing his weapon would blow his cover with her.

As Cecelia made the call, Holt evaluated each man, looking for a weakness he could exploit quickly so they could get out of here before agents, authorities or helpful citizens decided to intervene.

The man with the knife was weaker, but wary. Holt feinted left, and the knife flashed wide of his hip. Holt kicked out and caught the man's knee, and the knife skidded away as the thug crumpled. Cecelia snatched up the weapon.

"Keep that one down," he told her. Neither he nor Cecelia would be here to give a report, but these two deserved a night in jail.

He heard shouts on the street and a siren in the distance. Time was running out for them to get away cleanly. Cecelia was too well known in the area and the last complication he needed was local law enforcement.

The man swung wild, panicking with Holt's resistance and the warning that cops were on the way, and the jagged green edge caught at Holt's coat, dragging at the sleeve. Following the motion, he used the taller man's momentum to carry his fist into the hard steel of the trash bin.

The man howled with pain, but Holt used a quick series of uppercuts into his gut, robbing him of air and instantly silencing him. While he clutched his stomach, gasping for air, Holt drove another roundhouse into his jaw. The attacker slumped to the pavement, unconscious.

Holt turned back to find Cecelia pressing a Taser to the other assailant's thigh. The lady was more prepared than he'd suspected. "Nice job. Let's go."

"But the police—"

"Can take care of it."

Sirens wailed closer and he caught the flash of lights. Just what he *didn't* need tonight: the fastest response time of Alexandria's finest. The longer he could prevent Cecelia from learning his real identity and purpose here, the better.

"Let's go. Your charity doesn't need this kind of bad publicity."

She gave him a strange look but she cooperated, rushing through the narrow lane to join the foot traffic on the next street.

They walked briskly for another block before he

flagged a cab and opened the door for her to slide in ahead of him. "Your place or mine?"

When she didn't immediately respond, he opened his mouth, ready to offer the address for the Plaza, but she surprised him.

"Yours."

He struggled not to fidget or show his surprise over her choice as he gave the address for the marina where he kept his boat moored.

What in bloody hell did he do now?

Chapter Six

Thomas jerked to attention when the phone rang in the outer office. He'd sent his assistant home hours ago, instead calling on Holt's assistant, Nadine, to fill in.

"The surveillance team on the line for you, sir," Nadine said.

She'd resisted and tried to make excuses for not staying, but he'd given her an ultimatum: cooperate or resign. Her decision confirmed Nadine wasn't the mole and she'd answered all of his questions about what Holt had been asking her to do.

Unfortunately for Thomas, she didn't know too much. Holt wasn't careless and he didn't rely on Nadine for all of his scheduling. Based on the information she did have, Thomas sent another Specialist to cover the few hours of reconnaissance Holt had asked Nadine to handle. The appointed observation target had been Cecelia's house.

Thomas picked up the phone when the call transferred. "Report."

"We've lost her, Director."

Thomas picked up the painted plaster paperweight on his desk and nearly heaved it at the door before remembering it was a long-ago handmade gift from his niece.

"What happened?"

"You know her GPS isn't working on her cell?"

"No surprise," he barked. "How the hell did you lose her in the first place?"

"Everything was fine. We picked her up when she left the Plaza. She met her friends on schedule, but she stayed after they left the bar."

"And?"

"She eventually left the bar with Deputy Director Holt."

Thomas fisted his hand around the phone. "Where did they go?"

He rubbed his forehead with his free hand, unsure what he wanted to hear. He had a hard time believing Holt would hurt Cecelia on a professional level, and yet Holt wasn't the dating type. At least he'd never dated someone like Cecelia before.

Not to mention that damned chatter about her being the target of a kidnapping attempt.

Damn it!

"They went to dinner at Ray's."

Thomas struggled to calm himself. "Best steaks in Old Town."

"Yes, sir. We uploaded pictures of two men loitering near the restaurant."

"I saw those." He'd been waiting over an hour for the facial recognition software to spit out something useful.

"One of them went inside about a half hour before Mrs. Manning and Holt came out."

"No one got any audio on the dinner?"

"Impossible, sir, unless we'd joined them at the table."

"Understood." Some logistics couldn't be out-maneuvered, especially on short notice. "Do we have anything?"

The Specialist on the other end of the line hesitated. "Not much. We have prints and faces on the two men who tried to steal your sister's purse as she walked back to her hotel."

"She was mugged?"

"No, sir. The assailants were subdued."

"Was she hurt? What about Holt?"

"I don't have a clear answer yet. As I said, we've lost her trail. By the time we hit the scene, the potential victims were gone and the assailants unconscious."

"You left them for the local police to deal with."

"Yes, sir. Seemed like the best option."

Thomas agreed. "So the man hired to kidnap

my sister might have just accomplished the job?"
It didn't help matters any that Holt had been highly
trained in evasion techniques and could effectively
disappear without a trace in less than an hour.

After Nadine had spilled her sketchy information, Thomas had gone through Holt's office with
a critical eye. An extra identity remained in Holt's
office safe, but Thomas knew there should have
been at least one more, and the cash earmarked
for emergencies was gone.

He wasn't prone to displays of temper, but he
was about to lose it this time. This was his sister
they'd lost. Every scattered bit of information he
had said she was likely in the clutches of a traitor.
A traitor with skills and a past no brother wanted
to think about.

"Do we have anything close to a lead?"

"No, sir. We're about to run down cab compa-
nies. It's the fastest way they could clear the area."

"Or the bus or—"

"No, we've hacked those cameras. She hasn't
boarded any of the shuttles or the metro."

It could be worse. That was the prime source
of his problem, knowing exactly how much worse
it could be. The betrayal cut deep. He had hand-
picked Emmett Holt to replace Lucas when he retired. How the hell could he have been so wrong
about a guy with a pristine record?

He let the two agents he'd put on her go do their

jobs. Nadine was monitoring the police scanner in the area, but he also tasked an analyst downstairs with the same job to make sure she didn't miss or withhold anything he needed to know.

His cell phone chimed with a new text message. He grabbed it, ready to chew Lia out for turning off her GPS and dodging the protective tail, only to see Casey's number on the display.

He dialed her number when he saw the message: Call when you can.

"Hello," he said warmly, trying not to let on that her mother was missing. "Did Levi's flight get in on time?"

"Yeah. We're great. Mom moved over to the hotel tonight."

"I know."

"Thought you might. Does the team in the van have any crime-scene equipment?"

"What van?"

"Mom says there's been a van parked in front of the Millers' place for days. She assumed they were here on your orders."

"It wasn't me." Damn it. What exactly had Holt put into motion?

"Levi and I can check it out."

She sounded too ready for action. "Wait. Just leave it alone. I'll have someone deal with the van. Why didn't you call the police if you need a crime tech?"

"Because we're not sure we have a crime."

"Explain."

Casey took a big breath that rushed across the line. "We found a bug in the kitchen, then searched the house and found two more. The office and the bedroom."

Thomas cringed at the implications of those positions. Cecelia didn't work with sensitive information in her current position at the CIA, but that would change if she made the switch to ops.

"Go on."

"It's just a hunch, but I think someone's been here. Obviously to plant the bugs, but I mean tonight, when I went to the airport to pick up Levi."

If someone had been in the house, why hadn't the Specialist he'd assigned reported anything? His first instinct was to get over there and take a look personally. He used his computer to message Nadine, asking her to get a status report.

"I'm probably overreacting. It's not like I can point to any one thing and say it's out of place, but I just feel like a few things have been searched. I sent Mom a text, but she hasn't replied yet."

His jaw clenched. Being kidnapped had a tendency to interfere with messaging capabilities. "Did you check the safe?"

"Yes. It's fine. I'm thinking we got home before they found it."

"Was anything missing or..." He didn't know

quite how to finish the question. Security clearances for the job were one thing, but no matter how much field experience an agent had, investigating family was different.

"Everything looked the same to me. Well, almost the same."

Thomas thought he recognized the problem. "Was her wedding ring in there?"

"Yeah," Casey replied softly.

He had noticed Cecelia wasn't wearing the ring. Obviously Casey hadn't. That was going to be hard for her even though she would want her mother to be happy and to move one with her life. "You okay?"

"Sure." She sniffled. "It's just weird she's moving on."

"Only she can know when it's time."

"Oh, please. Don't try and go all wise on me. I know it bugs you, too."

"A little," he admitted. William had been like a brother, but he was gone now. Cecelia deserved to live the rest of her life. Just not like this.

Mostly because it was Holt. That wasn't entirely true. Up until a few weeks ago, Holt had his utmost respect. Now, as Thomas peeled back the layers on cases going back to June, he was starting to get a picture of a very different man. A man who was in bed with a very dangerous enemy.

Isely had every reason to hate Thomas, and it

appeared he had bottomless resources to fund the revenge he'd promised years ago. The financial picture was still coming in, but it was clear Isely's deals since taking over the family business had been savvy, private and lucrative.

"Your mom's smart. She'll find her way. The best thing we can do is keep supporting her." He hoped he hadn't already let her down.

"Right. You've got her covered tonight?"

"Sure thing," he lied. How in the hell was he going to fix this?

"I'm meeting her late tomorrow morning. We have a mini spa thing at the Plaza."

"Sounds good. Can Levi stay at the house? Keep it covered in case whoever planted those bugs comes back?"

"We already decided that was best."

"Great minds," Thomas said. "Enjoy the rest of your evening."

"We will. See you tomorrow night, Uncle Thomas."

"Can't wait."

Thomas stared at the phone when the call ended. He should get out to Alexandria, but something—that gut instinct he'd learned to trust—told him to wait.

Instead, he called in a favor with the local police. They could check on any cars that didn't belong in Cecelia's neighborhood. Then he picked up his cell phone and called his wife to give her an update on the degrading situation.

Hearing her voice would be the only thing good about this night.

Chapter Seven

The marina? It was just one more question on the list spinning through Cecelia's mind, none of which she wanted him to answer here in the cab.

She didn't need the echoes of her brother's warning to reach the obvious conclusion that Emmett Holt wasn't some average guy with a private security firm, as he'd posted in his online profile. The surprise attack and resulting tension between them made it clear they both knew there was more going on here.

"Are you hurt?"

He didn't reply, just sat beside her, his body rigid, his hands on his knees. His eyes, she knew, were scouring the street, looking for any sign they were being followed.

Adjusting her purse, she reached over and laced her fingers through his. He startled, then stared. First at their joined hands, then slowly he lifted his glacier gaze to meet hers.

"I'm a good listener," she said, low enough that

the cab driver wouldn't overhear. She told herself that this was part of what a good field agent would do...but she wasn't entirely sure that was the motive for her actions.

She prayed she wasn't being a fool.

Still, of all the things she might have told him, that one point seemed the most relevant. It didn't make sense. He'd obviously lied to her about a few things, but something about the man beside her—the frown twisting his face, the tension in his body—made her say that first.

She had the odd feeling he was in over his head. As a deputy director of an elite covert team, it didn't seem entirely reasonable. Her brother's team of Specialists was well trained to salvage ops that slid sideways and out of reach. Their success rate was ridiculously high because Thomas wouldn't tolerate anything less. What could possibly worry a man with that kind of experience and expertise?

The potential answers didn't offer any sort of comfort. Just the opposite.

Remembering how one attacker had demanded *her,* she shivered. Her apparent savior shifted, tucking her under the shelter of his arm. She should tell him those same men had asked her for directions just a few hours ago, should tell him she knew who he was. She should tell him about the message Casey had sent a few minutes ago.

But she couldn't bring herself to say any of

those things in the cab. "Thank you," she said, as the post-adrenaline tremors set in.

He rubbed her shoulder and pressed a kiss to her hair. It wasn't the kind of gesture she expected from a worldly operative or a man supposedly betraying his team and country. There was an inherent kindness behind the comfort he offered her.

"You did well," he said.

Not from her perspective. "You did all the hard work." She traced the rip in his jacket sleeve. "It's ruined."

"It's replaceable."

"We should have a real conversation."

"Probably," he said, twisting a bit to peer out the back window.

"Will we?"

He didn't reply, just squeezed her shoulder once more.

Her tremors eased up as the cab driver turned into the marina entrance. The landscaping on either side of the drive was draped with colorful holiday lights, but it didn't do anything to lift her mood.

A loud party overflowed the marina building and she did a mental rundown of the local calendar, trying to figure out if she'd know anyone attending, but she couldn't recall who had rented the space for tonight.

Would she call out for help anyway? Or just

keep going with the flow and hoping this man was the hero she wanted him to be?

Maybe her daughter and brother were right. Maybe she didn't have the right stuff for this kind of work.

"Looks like quite a bash going down," the cab driver observed as Emmett paid the fare.

"Sailors always know how to party," he agreed. "Thanks for the lift."

Instead of leading her around toward the water, he guided her straight toward the raucous party. "We're not dressed for this kind of event," she protested.

He looked her up and down and the resulting shiver had nothing to do with fear or adrenaline. Only anticipation. "Not every party is a gala." The wind caught her hair, but he smoothed it back behind her ear. "You look very good to me."

And he looked pretty damned gorgeous, even after the fight in a grimy alley. At this point she wanted answers. He had a point, though. The safety of a friendly crowd held a good deal of appeal just now. "We need to talk."

"We will. I promise." His mouth thinned to a grim line. "As soon as we're safe." He urged her closer to the front doors.

"What's going on? What did those men want?" Besides her.

"We'll figure that out," he promised, "as soon as we know we're not being followed anymore."

Since those two men had been stalking her before the encounter in the alley, she couldn't actually blame him for what happened. Truth was, he had saved her from God only knew what sort of fate. For now, she had no choice but to trust him.

"I thought you gave this address because you had a boat here," she murmured as they checked their coats and prepared to join the revelers inside.

"Even if I do have a boat here, I'm not going to lead whoever followed us right to it."

Spy 101, she mused as she looked over his shoulder. "I don't see anyone."

"Doesn't mean they aren't out there."

Now, that sounded ominous. And more than a little paranoid. But she could tell he was sincerely concerned about the likelihood of more trouble. And he was highly trained. Like Thomas.

"Then we should go to the police."

"Not yet."

She refused to take another step. "Why not?"

"Trust me. I'll explain later." He took her elbow and urged her forward again. "Come on, it's time to blend in and get festive."

She pushed a hand through her hair and tugged at her sweater. From the guests they'd passed already, she knew it wasn't black tie, but she got the impression it was a private company event. "You're serious about crashing."

"As a heart attack." He held up the tag from the coat check and gave her a look she knew was meant to put an end to her balking. "Just to buy some time."

The man looked around the room as if the crowd had taken over his home uninvited. "We won't blend in at all if you keep doing that," she warned.

"Doing what?"

"Scowling. It's not *festive*." She circled a finger at his face. "We're crashing a party and you look like you're on the way to your execution. Try a smile." She gave him an example.

His first attempt—a grimace—actually scared her a little. She glanced over his shoulder at the door. "Relax. They were just a couple of muggers," she said, though neither of them believed it. "We weren't followed."

So far. She mentally crossed her fingers as she drew him deeper into the anonymity of the party and joined the line waiting for service at the bar.

"Not smart," he grumbled at her ear.

"Look around." Everyone carried some sort of drink. "This was your idea. You want to blend," she said with a wink. She swayed provocatively to the music pounding through the room. "And those thugs interrupted us before we got to dance."

She hoped a drink and a dance would be enough

to stop the ruination of what had started as a perfectly lovely evening. Keeping it simple, she ordered a beer for each of them and then led him to a spot just off the dance floor. If this was really some sort of operation that involved her, this was the perfect time to prove she had what it took for fieldwork.

She clinked her beer bottle to his. "Happy holidays."

"Cheers." He tipped the bottle back, but kept his eyes on hers.

In the improved light of the party, she could see the red abrasions on his knuckles. They'd likely be dark bruises by morning. "Do you want ice for that?" She wondered how he'd managed not to break any bones.

"I'm good." He rubbed the cold bottle across the marred skin while he studied the crowd.

"Yes, you were." She stepped a bit closer. "Thank you, by the way."

"You said that already." He frowned at her, but she decided it was because she wasn't what he expected. Well, that made them even. "You certainly adapt quickly."

"I've—"

"Mrs. Manning?"

"The woman knows everyone in town," he grumbled.

Cecelia found herself in the exuberant, slightly

tipsy embrace of a young woman who'd gone to school with Casey.

"Merry Christmas, Heather." Too late, Cecelia remembered the invitation she'd declined. Heather's father was a broker and their girls had been on the varsity field hockey team in high school. William had made a few investments with him, but they weren't particularly close friends.

"I didn't know Daddy invited you. Oh, my gosh!" She stepped back, eyed Cecelia up and down. "You look amazing!"

"You're too kind."

"Daddy is going to go nuts." Heather leaned close, but didn't lower her voice. "He's always had a thing for you." She put her hand over her lips. "Oops."

Cecelia cringed at the dark expression clouding Emmett's eyes. "Heather, let me introduce you to my *date,* Mr. Holt."

He did a fine job pretending to enjoy the introduction, but Cecelia knew better. His gaze was cataloging faces and he was looking for ways to make a hasty exit.

"Anyway, I'm so glad you came," Heather effused.

The music changed to a Latin beat and Emmett captured her hand. "Let's dance," he said, pushing their beer bottles toward Heather. She barely had time to wave a farewell to the younger woman as Emmett tugged her into the crowd of dancers.

His hands molded to her hips; his touch burned with a hot purpose through the fabric of her slacks as he started to lead. She grinned and rested her hands lightly on his shoulders for balance. Already she realized this wasn't a ballroom rendition of the salsa he had in mind, but something much more intense. Sexy.

Something much more fun.

Thank heaven the party guests were drinking heavily enough that they wouldn't remember Mrs. Manning crashing the party and grinding it out with a stranger in public.

She couldn't help it. Blaming the adrenaline or just her eagerness to reclaim her life, she tossed her head back and laughed at the absurdity of it all. She had to play the part, didn't she? Wasn't this exactly what spies did in the field?

When she met his gaze again, his half smile was full of a different kind of heat. A heat that made her want to take chances and explore their options, no matter who he was or how many interruptions they had to endure.

For the past three weeks, he'd been charming her with clever, interesting emails and photographs of architecture and sailing—his two passions outside work, according to his profile. That had been enough to captivate her even before she'd realized his profile picture had been current—and incredibly accurate.

The man was a walking—dancing—invitation to sin. Right now she should be insisting on finding a quiet corner and getting some real answers, but she couldn't pull her head out of the sexy spell he was weaving around her.

The logical part of her brain knew he was doing it on purpose. An applied technique for either protection or distraction, she wasn't sure. Wasn't even sure she wanted the answer just yet. Instead of being terrified by the near miss in the alley, she felt exhilarated. There was an energy Emmett drew out of her that she hadn't felt in far too long.

More than surviving, more than managing life, she realized she was really living again—for the moment.

The revelation would have made her stumble, but Emmett was there. His hands guided her, brushed her body as they swiveled and rocked in time with the fast pulse of the music.

He used his eyes to tell her they'd been followed, and turning her, she spotted a pair of burly men hovering at the sliding door that opened onto the wide deck. They must have come around from the dockside rather than the front door as she and Emmett had done. With their well-worn coats and rough clothing, they didn't blend in with anyone other than the two men who'd attacked them in the alley.

She did a slow turn to face him again, then leaned in close on the next forward step. "Plan?"

"I'm thinking."

Step, sway, forward, back. Cecelia laid her palms on his. "We can't let them start a fight here. People will get hurt."

"I know," he growled.

"They said they wanted me."

"Yes."

"Want to hand me over?"

"No. Unless you know something I don't."

She shook her head. "Kiss me."

"What?"

Her idea was flimsy at best, but it was all they had. The bad guys wanted her. She could be bait, especially with Emmett ready to assist her.

Her heart stumbled at the thoughts. Was she really ready to do this? Play bait…and kiss this man?

"Kiss me when the dance ends. Make a scene out of it." The dance carried them apart for a moment, then back again. "I'll go to the restroom. If they follow, we can subdue them there and leave through the back door."

He didn't look happy about it. Apparently, no one wanted to credit her with any skills beyond marriage, motherhood and pushing paper. It wasn't her first brush with disbelief, but there would be plenty of time to deal with her bruised pride later.

Besides, she had a lifetime of hearing William, Thomas and more recently, Casey, talk about how to execute a proper egress in the most unusual of circumstances.

The music soared as the song ended and Emmett put a flourish on the last move, dipping her back over his arm and bringing her back up so fast in the next beat that her head spun. Then his mouth captured hers.

His fingers speared into her hair, his palm hot, firm and somehow gentle where he cradled her head. She gripped his shoulders for balance, digging into his firm muscles when he shifted, taking the kiss deeper. His thigh wedged between hers, his other hand splayed across her back.

Her breath stalled in her lungs, but she didn't care. She'd told him to make a scene and he was doing a fine job of it. His tongue stroked boldly against hers, making dark, silky promises her body wanted him to keep.

The cheers and catcalls brought her back to reality with a shock. He released her so suddenly she swayed. She touched her lips, staring at him a long moment before remembering she was supposed to make a break for the restrooms.

He drew her body close to his and she had the wild hope he would kiss her again.

"Go," he whispered against her cheek as the next song started.

Cecelia went. Like the hounds of hell were on her heels. Within seconds she heard heavy footfalls behind her as she rounded the corner. On a prayer the restroom might be empty, she pushed through the door into the ladies' room and spun a quick circle in search of anything she could use as a weapon. She should have gone back into that alley for her Taser. She'd dropped it after putting that creep down. She'd never had to use it before.

If she couldn't Taser a guy without being shaken, how was she ever going to fire a weapon?

"Focus, Cecelia," she muttered. She needed a weapon. Nothing presented itself, and she knew her best bet was to barricade herself in one of the stalls and wait for Emmett.

She scrambled into a stall, set the latch and climbed onto the closed toilet seat. As the two men barreled in, Cecelia peered through the crack in the stall door and nearly groaned when a young woman stepped out of the stall closest to the door. *Heather.*

"Uh, wrong door, guys."

"Where is Mrs. Manning?"

These two knew her name? Any lingering notion she'd harbored that the attack after dinner had been a random mugging or a case of mistaking her for another woman fled. Not that she'd really believed it, even at the time.

"Not in here. You guys are at the wrong party," Heather added, trying to get around the men to the sink. "Get out."

One of the men caught Heather's arm hard enough to make her cry out.

"Show yourself, Manning."

Dear Lord. Cecelia couldn't let them hurt the younger woman. "Let her go," she said, stepping out of the last stall.

"Come with us. Now," the other man ordered.

"As soon as you let her go," Cecelia repeated with far more calm than she felt.

The man holding Heather pulled a gun and pressed it to Heather's side. The girl paled. "We all go together."

"Not acceptable." Cecelia inched closer to the next stall, judging the reach of the second man. *Come on, Emmett.* None of the self-defense moves she knew were applicable from this distance. She had to find a way to get Heather away from that gun.

"Last warning," Cecelia promised. "Let. Her. Go." She took a step closer with each word and on the last she let the second man catch her arm. She resisted and then suddenly gave in when he pulled harder. The result brought her careening into his chest and the momentum carried them both into his partner.

The four of them landed in a heap against the wall with Cecelia on top. The gun, thank God, had fallen closest to her. She stomped and punched on every sensitive area possible as she scrambled to her feet.

"Run, Heather!"

Heather obeyed, bolting through the open doorway as Emmett rushed in and Cecelia grabbed the gun.

"Can I just shoot them?" Maybe the weapon part wouldn't be as difficult as she'd thought. What kind of lowlifes would use a young woman as leverage?

"Works for me."

Both men started to protest. Cecelia glanced at Emmett and her heart skipped when he smiled at her.

"Do me a favor and just kneecap them," he suggested.

She adjusted her aim and the men shouted again until Emmett silenced each with precisely placed pressure on the carotid artery.

"We should get you out of here."

"Will you tell me what the hell is going on?" she demanded.

"Just as soon as I figure it out," he said, handing her coat to her.

Emmett searched the unconscious pair for identification while she shrugged into her coat. He examined their phones and wallets as she dropped the small revolver into her purse. If she hadn't been watching him closely, she would have missed the quick move when he put a phone from his jacket into the pocket of one of the men.

With more questions begging to be asked, she followed him out of the restroom, down the corridor and out the back door of the building. If Heather had rushed out to call the police, it hadn't stopped the partying.

If someone had asked her, Cecelia wouldn't have been able to logically justify her decision to stick with Emmett as he led her away and toward the water. The sounds of the party faded, replaced by the soothing lap of water against the moorings and their soft, rapid steps on the planks of the gangway.

Darkness enveloped them beneath the low glow of the sparsely placed lamps marking the intersections of the gangway with the narrow floating docks that stretched out toward the water.

Emmett took her hand, steadying her as they turned down the last dock. Boats rocked gently in the slips on either side. If he had been sent to kidnap her, she was making it easy for him. But she couldn't make herself believe that was his goal. He'd had ample opportunity and offers to let others do it for him. No, there was more going on here, and as soon as she knew they were safe, she was going to demand answers.

He stopped abruptly and pressed a finger to her lips. "You have the gun?"

She nodded.

"Good." He withdrew his finger. "Sit here and use it if you have to."

"Where are you going?"

"Just wait here while I make sure it's clear."

"I could run," she pointed out.

That stopped him. He turned back slowly. "Do you want to?"

The edge in his voice—sharper than that broken bottle—was enough to make her grateful she couldn't see what was surely a cold expression marring his handsome face.

"No." Not yet, she amended silently. She could only assume the men who had attacked them were working for Thomas's enemy. That was the only explanation that made sense.

But that only proved her brother's point that his enemy couldn't have found *her* without access to highly classified files. Files that technically didn't exist. Files a deputy director could access easily.

"Let's go."

She jumped and nearly dropped the revolver she'd balanced on her knee. He'd returned in complete silence; the dock hadn't even shifted. "How'd you do that?"

"Practice." His hand cupped her elbow. "Three steps down," he advised when he paused again at a slip.

She couldn't see much beyond the general shape of the boat and she took the steps slowly in the dark. The boat rocked slightly beneath her feet with her third step.

"Left," he said, guiding her with his strong hands.

Looking that way, she saw a sliver of light seeping through a thin crack of a hatch near the boat's bow. She felt him next to her, a bundle of tension and heat, his intriguing scent mingling with the water and night.

"Just follow me. You're safe. You have my word."

His voice, his touch, both made her *feel* safe. But was she?

With one hand on the gun in her pocket, she followed him farther into the dark, wondering what the hell she'd gotten herself into. In reality, she didn't have a choice here. What she had was an opportunity. An opportunity to help her brother and the CIA take down a traitor.

And maybe to prove she wasn't a total fool.

She prayed she wasn't a total fool.

Chapter Eight

After securing the door, Holt watched Cecelia turn a slow circle, taking in the quarters of his modest cruiser, and waited for the disappointment. He should have known she'd be too polite to let it show.

"It's gorgeous," she said, sounding breathless.

"Thanks," he muttered. He didn't believe her. His boat wasn't gorgeous, it was simple. Sure, he'd chosen the finest materials when he'd done the necessary upgrades, but the streamlined design made the most of space best described as cramped. It hadn't bothered him before because he hadn't planned to ever share these quarters with anyone. Seeing her here had him questioning his solitary plans, which was a completely random and impossible line of thinking.

She was the director's sister and a potential victim he was trying to protect by pretending to date her. Key word: *pretending*. He had to keep that in mind.

"Were you sailing on this when you took those pictures down along the Florida Keys?" She moved about the space, touching his things. His body reacted as if she were touching him.

"That's where I picked her up," he said. It surprised him how much pleasure he got from her enthusiasm for the boat and the pictures he'd taken. Sailing wasn't in her online profile and his searches hadn't revealed any recent love of the sea, but by now he should expect the unexpected where Cecelia Manning was concerned.

Holt rarely encountered anyone who surprised him as much as this beautiful woman. She was nervous about being here alone with him. But she'd come willingly. That said, she still clutched the weapon in her pocket.

"You can let go of the gun. I'm not stealing you away." Not tonight, anyway. Based on Isely's behavior, it looked like tomorrow was still task one on the agenda.

She visibly attempted to relax, withdrawing her hand from her pocket but leaving the weapon there in case she needed it. As if she knew what the move did to him, she ran her newly freed hand along the polished teak of the cabinetry.

Holt had to look away. His imagination painted a vivid picture of her hands running over his skin with the same blatant appreciation.

Wasn't going to happen. Not once she knew the

truth. Hell, she probably already knew more than she should. Focus, man. He needed a change of clothes. To get the grime of thugs off him.

"It's so warm."

He stopped in the process of emptying his pockets onto the narrow table, certain he hadn't heard her correctly. "Pardon me?"

"The cabin," she said. "I would have expected it to be cold down here."

Ah, that made more sense and was a complete departure from where his thoughts had traveled. "Yeah. That's part of the design." He opened the laptop he kept on board and inserted a flash drive. "I'll get you back to your hotel just as soon as I check out a few things." Primarily that it would be safe to take her there. Highly unlikely, but he had an obligation to check.

"No rush. It's nice to just breathe for a moment."

"You should call your brother and let him know you're safe."

Holt didn't like the look she sent his way but he ignored it, putting his energy into gaining some insight about Isely's inexplicable escalation. If she hadn't known who he was before, she'd certainly already figured out plenty about him.

"So you do know who I am. Who I'm related to."

"I know you're Cecelia Manning. Recently widowed, philanthropist and your slice backhand is the best shot of your tennis game. You enjoy time with friends, your weekly yoga class and prefer pinot noir to merlot."

"The wine thing wasn't on my profile."

Time to face the music. There was no more time for games. "No, I learned that by perusing your wine rack."

"You've been in my *house?*"

The astonishment on her face sucker punched him. He gritted his teeth for a second then said the rest. "Easier to plant the bugs that way."

"You bugged my house." She swore softly, but with enough heat that he knew her cooperation was over.

He'd just have to deal with that. Better to clear the air here and now so they could be on the same page moving forward. She might hate him for his tactics, but he couldn't leave her alone now. Not with Isely's erratic behavior. Holt opened his mouth, but her clear, regal voice filled the galley instead.

"Thomas did put you up to this. I'm going to kill him with my bare hands," she finished with a low growl. "He's getting better at lying to me. There was a time when he would never have been able to pull something like this over on me."

Her statement about Casey gave him pause. "No. Wait. You can tell when he's lying?" It was something Holt still hadn't mastered and a skill that would be useful beyond measure. Assuming he managed to keep his job.

"Apparently not anymore," she glared at him, then she bit her lip and her eyes shimmered with unshed tears.

"Don't do that." He could not deal with a weepy woman tonight. Not any time.

Less than half an hour ago, she'd danced like they'd never been jumped in the alley. Her eyes had been clear when she'd agreed to kneecap the assailants at the party if necessary. Why would learning their connection had been a setup distress her so?

"Don't worry. I won't crumple." She gazed upward and blinked rapidly. "I'm just angry."

An unexpected emotion nudged him. Guilt. "You're wrong. Sort of. Thomas had nothing to do with this. Unless you told him, he doesn't know about us."

"Us?" She gave a short, brittle laugh.

"Us." He forgot the mission and the phones and reached across the small cabin for her, realizing he'd lose her cooperation completely if he didn't handle this right. Her cooperation was critical in these next hours, even if Thomas didn't understand that yet. If she broke down in a panic or flew off in a rage, Isely would have her—and use her against the two most knowledgeable agents in Mission Recovery.

She shrugged him off, but there was nowhere for her to go. He wrapped his arms around her waist, holding her close until she stopped struggling. "Just let me explain."

"You lied to me. All these weeks." Tears threatened again, but she prevailed. "I'm an idiot."

"No, you're not. I lie to everyone. It's part of the job, and I'm very good at my job."

She blew out a sharp breath that shifted her bangs out of her eyes. "I know. I know."

"From what I hear, you'll be joining the ranks of people like me next month."

She rolled her eyes. "Of course a man in your position could find that out."

"Are you excited about the move to ops?"

She scowled up at him, clearly unwilling to change the subject. Wisps of her hair were tangled at the corner of her long lashes and he cautiously moved them to the side.

At least the tears were gone and she looked like her composed self again. And mad as hell.

"Thomas said someone wants to kidnap me."

Holt nodded. "That he was right about that should be obvious after two attacks in as many hours."

"He mentioned your name."

Holt stiffened. "Good."

Those lake-blue eyes of hers went wide. "Good?"

"That's what I need him to believe." He took

in the clenched teeth. "His warning is why you thought about ditching me at the bar." That last part was a guess, but coming to that conclusion was fairly easy.

She sniffed, clearly annoyed he'd deduced correctly. "And just what am I supposed to believe, Mr. Holt?"

There was an easy answer, but he couldn't get the words past his lips. Lips that wanted to taste hers again and show her the honest, brutal need for her beating like a drum inside him.

To preserve his sanity, he released her and took a step back. To seal the deal on her continued cooperation he said what he needed to say. "When I learned you might be a target, I used the online profile to get closer. Thomas doesn't know anything about my approach, and I'm sure he'd be furious to know how much I've come to care for you."

She scoffed, turning her back on him and tracing the wave design carved into the cabinet door. "He said I was a pawn."

"To his enemy, you are."

"But not to you."

He should clarify, admit the confusion twisting inside his gut where she was concerned, but they were short on time. On some level what he said wasn't a lie. But this was new territory for him, these emotions unfamiliar. This was no time to be confused. He slid onto the bench at the table and set out the phones he'd taken from Isely's men.

Rather than dwell on the confusion, he focused on the facts. "The team Thomas assigned to follow you is in a world of hurt about now. Please send him a text that you're okay and safely in your room."

"I should." She pulled out her phone, tapping it against her open palm. "No matter what I tell him, he'll only follow the GPS signal here."

"You disabled that before you left the hotel to meet me."

She gave him a startled look, but didn't deny it. "For the date that wasn't," she groused.

"I think it would've been a great night if we'd been left alone."

"Maybe," she allowed.

"Why'd you do it?"

"The GPS or the date?"

"The GPS." Though he'd be lying to himself if he didn't admit he would very much like it if she answered both questions.

She shrugged. "Thomas likes a challenge. I assume he recruits like-minded people."

Holt laughed at her accurate assumption. "Here I thought it was because you were ashamed to be seen with me."

She leaned back against the woodwork she'd admired and did something with her phone before dumping it back in her purse. She drummed her fingers lightly as she watched him.

He didn't care for the close study, but he managed to ignore it.

"I was never ashamed to meet you. Not even after Thomas warned me off. I was curious. Excited," she admitted. "And not at all ready to share you with my overprotective family or nosy friends. I was determined to prove that Thomas was wrong about you. I'm reassessing that conclusion just now."

"Are you always so candid?" He started downloading the text messages and recent locations logged by the system since the phones were activated.

"No."

He counted himself fortunate in that much, at least. "How did you plan to explain my appearance tomorrow night?"

"Vaguely."

She was smiling, he could hear it in her voice. It worried him. Not the smile specifically, but recognizing her inflections so well already. Not recognizing, he amended, reacting to. That was the issue here. Recognizing what others were thinking was his job. Reacting this way to anyone was not.

"What are you doing?"

"Reviewing communications," he said. Then an idea occurred to him. Cecelia didn't like her brother and daughter doubting her. "Want to help?"

"Sure."

She slid onto the bench beside him and the hint of vanilla in her perfume tugged at his senses. The scent was one he associated with innocence, but the images she inspired were in no way innocent. Having her join him had been a mistake. A rookie mistake. He hadn't made one of those since he'd actually been a rookie. He handed her a phone and told her to run through the call log and text messages.

"We'll take out the SIM cards and toss the phones on our way to the hotel."

"*Our* way?"

"There's no way I'm letting you out of my sight. They'd have you in less than a minute."

"I'm not that easy."

"No, you're not. But they *are* that good."

"Thomas thinks you're working with them. I get the impression they think you're working with them."

Ah, more of that refreshing frankness. He slid down the bench and away so he could gather the few things he needed. He didn't reply to her fishing comment.

"Oh, I get it. That's what they're supposed to believe."

"You're a quick study. Can you finish this while I pack?"

"If you tell me what I'm looking for."

"You'll know it when you see it. One-word messages. Addresses. There's probably nothing incriminating anyway, but I want to try."

His laptop and tuxedo were already at the room he'd booked under an alias at the Plaza, but he wanted a change of clothes, his camera and the money and gun he knew would trace back to Isely's illegal operation.

"Emmett?"

"Yeah?"

"Who is Irina?"

The name wasn't familiar to him. "Could be a contact."

"Hmm. There's a date listed in the next message." She nudged the phone across the table to show him the text message. "It's this Saturday."

The day after the gala where Isely had ordered him to kidnap her. He thought of the warehouse address he'd received at the restaurant. A warehouse on the water would be the perfect staging area and make it easy for Isely to take Cecelia out of the country.

"What are the other numbers?" she asked.

He looked. "Best guess is latitude and longitude." As specific as an address could be, Holt thought with more than a little frustration for not anticipating an exchange at sea. Without a deeper investigation into the name listed, he couldn't make assumptions.

"But—"

He cut her off. "We can analyze it later." He made sure the information was downloaded, then closed the computer and tucked the SIM cards into his camera bag. "For now we have to get you back to the hotel without being intercepted by your brother or Isely's crew."

"Sounds like fun."

He stared at her, caught the sparkle in her eyes. "You're serious."

She nodded. "I'll think of it as an early training exercise."

"Except this is real and your life is in danger."

"Seems like mine isn't the only one. You appear to have a few enemies of your own."

"A few more now since I didn't hand you over to Isely's men tonight."

"Why does he want me?"

"So he can cause your brother pain." But he was starting to suspect there was more going on in Isely's mind than just his determination to destroy Thomas's family and reputation.

"What did Thomas do?"

"His job."

Holt doused the lights in the cabin, relieved when the darkness seemed to mute Cecelia, as well. She was asking too many questions he wasn't ready to answer.

Tomorrow night, when he was sure the two of

them were away cleanly, he'd tell her everything. He was counting on her to understand and be willing to do what was necessary to save her brother and the Mission Recovery team from disaster.

She didn't know it yet, but after witnessing her courage tonight, she'd become the ace up his sleeve. Her initiative gave him hope they both might yet get out of this in one piece.

The boat rocked gently in the slip as they moved up on deck. "We have to get out of here before the local police start searching the docks." Not to mention Isely's goons.

"You're sure the police can't help us?" she asked.

He steadied her as she took the wide step across the dark water to the dock. They moved quietly toward the gangway. "I'm the bad guy, remember? More to the point, people in our line of work are supposed to avoid getting caught."

"We can't just sail away?"

"I wish," he muttered. "Too many people know you around here. They'll send a unit to your house as soon as your friends at the party mention your name."

"Maybe that's a good thing. My daughter sent a text earlier. She thought someone had been in the house while she'd gone to the airport."

"Was anything missing?"

She shook her head. "It's probably nothing, just her uncle's concern for me weighing on her mind.

Police involvement will only aggravate Thomas. He's had a team parked on my street, watching the house, for days."

Holt considered telling her the observation team hadn't been sent by Thomas, but it could wait. He was more concerned about the break-in at her house. One more wrinkle in an op he might never iron out the way he wanted to.

She paused just outside the soft glow of the light where the dock met the gangway. "There's no way the police won't be looking for me. Heather witnessed those men attempting to take me. I should just go into the marina and give a statement. I can prove you were there to help me."

"Not a good idea. I wish we could prove you weren't even there."

"Too many camera phones for that to work," she said, sounding weary for the first time.

Holt pulled out the remaining functional burner phone and called the cab company.

"You have the number memorized?"

"I saw it on the dash of the cab on the way here," he said.

"You have a photographic memory?"

He nodded. "The one good discovery from my childhood." Why had he said that? His childhood had no significance here, aside from the street smarts he'd learned that might help them. "I don't think your brother has turned over my name yet. Any friends on the police force?"

"Of course."

"Of course," he echoed. "You have friends everywhere. Call one of them. Give him some line about gala business and offer to give your statement at the hotel." He checked his watch. "In an hour."

"It's a twenty-minute drive."

"Let's hope so."

"What should I say about you?"

"Nothing if you can get away with it. If you have to say something, call me protective detail. That should hold up for a day or two."

"Then what?"

"By then, if this isn't fixed, we'll probably both have bigger problems than leaving things out of a police report."

He handed her the ball cap he'd brought from the boat. "Put your hair up and keep your head down. Button your purse inside your coat." She gave him a questioning glance and he explained, "Changes your shape."

"The cab is meeting us two blocks south of the marina."

"You know, we could just walk back to Old Town."

He stared at her. "It's an option. As is stealing the car Isely's team used to get here."

"Did you take the keys?"

"Yeah." He patted his pocket and withdrew the key, tossing it out into the water. "It would be a mistake. If the police aren't on it, Isely will be tracking it."

Her gaze fell to the slice in his coat. "The cab it is."

Action decided, he guided her away from the water. They walked quickly toward the marina, keeping to the grassy areas cast in shadows, far away from the disrupted party.

"What do I say if someone stops us?"

"Accuse me of kidnapping and plead for help."

"But you—"

"Make a scene," he suggested as she had earlier. "Consider it good practice. This won't be the first tough choice you make in ops," he said. "Ditching me is an easy call. Trust me, I'm used to it."

Chapter Nine

Cecelia knew she would never just ditch him. She might not entirely understand what he was up to, but she didn't believe he was out to hurt her or that he was really working against Thomas. If she'd had any doubts, they had vanished almost completely when he'd risked himself to protect her from those men. She made the call to her friend on the police force.

When she put the phone away, her nerves were evident from her rapid, foggy vapor-cloud breaths in the cold night air. It was obvious enough that Emmett quietly instructed her to cover her mouth and nose with her scarf. It made her feel a bit like a train robber from the Wild West, but it worked. She appreciated the pointer.

She studied the way he moved, his effective blending of confidence and caution, and tried to emulate it as they slipped away from the marina. The flashing lights and distressed voices of partygoers faded behind them as they walked down to meet the cab.

When they were once more in the relative safety of the cab, she pulled down her scarf and grinned up at him. This kind of thing probably wasn't supposed to feel like fun, but it was so much better than sitting at her desk watching her life tick by.

The part of her that rebelled at the thought of ditching him was positively giddy that it hadn't come to that. She understood the logic of his plan, but it was the flash of grief in his eyes when he'd admitted he was used to it that bothered her. Whoever had left him somewhere in his past had scarred him in the process.

It made her angry on his behalf, made her want to let him know some people could be trusted to do the right thing. That was a concept he should know from working with her brother's covert team, but she knew from William that a sense of isolation was a frequent result of long-term undercover operations.

The man was a loner. Most spies were, for obvious reasons, but she got the sense that he'd been that way long before her brother had recruited him to Mission Recovery.

"How did you land such a great job?"

She knew from the hard line of his mouth and cocked eyebrow he understood exactly what she meant. She could also see he didn't want to tell her.

"Standard first-date question," she teased, catching the smile on the driver's face reflected in the rearview mirror. He wanted her to sell one picture to anyone the cops might find and question, but after he'd saved her—twice—she was determined to sell another version of their story.

He'd behaved admirably all night—the perfect gentleman and valiant defender. However he'd managed to raise Thomas's suspicions, she knew it wasn't as simple as Thomas might believe.

"Fair enough." He rubbed his hands together, blowing on them as if he was chilled. "I'd finished a rather delicate piece of work during an internship in New York City. It caught some attention and a recruiter arrived. It took some convincing, but eventually I made the change."

She knew how to read between the lines, to sort fact from necessary fiction, but usually she had a frame of reference. With Emmett, she only had the online dating profile and the knowledge that he'd been trained to lie, to adapt to the cover story when necessary and make it believable.

One day soon, assuming she survived whatever *this* was, she'd be doing the same thing.

She'd seen many resumes cross her desk at the office, and she understood the natural language that bolstered rather average accomplishments. With Emmett, she sensed the reverse was true. His self-reliance and swagger wasn't all show. It was a direct result of practice becoming a string of successes.

She'd married William so young. It gave her the unique perspective of watching him change through the course of his career, especially in the early years. Those had been some rough days, being a wife and stay-at-home mother while learning how to read a husband who couldn't discuss his day without breaking security protocols.

"A delicate piece of work" could mean anything, which meant New York might be the kernel of truth. Or the whole story might be completely false.

Emmett surprised her by taking her hand in his. "I like my job and I've enjoyed my time with the company. It's been good work."

Said like a man who didn't think he'd be at it much longer. Already he was putting Mission Recovery in the past tense.

Indirectly, her husband and daughter had taught her more than she realized, including the inherent risks of working with an agent with a fatalistic attitude.

She shouldn't be thinking about snooping into his past. As much as she tried, she couldn't even come up with a good reason to do so. The kiss—as stunning as it was—didn't count. Her friends from the grief-counseling group would probably say she was transferring her feelings for William to Emmett. Except she'd never confessed to them she didn't have the capacity for that depth of feeling anymore.

Logically, the feelings she was experiencing tonight were most likely due to her innate need to nurture and fix. And to show her appreciation for his protection, of course.

As the cab pulled up to the hotel, she wondered if her motives really mattered. Her brother said she was a target and Emmett had proved his determination to keep her safe. She had to consider the possibility his effort was a ruse to get her to lower her guard, but she was willing to give him the benefit of the doubt. For tonight, anyway.

"Go on and give your statement," he said, nudging her to the front door. "I'll be upstairs. You know how to find me."

She didn't watch him go, didn't need the distraction of his body right now. She was smart enough to know setups happened, but through her years as a wife and mother she'd learned to trust her intuition.

There was more to Emmett Holt than he showed, and her instincts said if he didn't open up to someone about his real mission, he was headed for a downfall. Cecelia pulled the cap from her head and ran her fingers through her hair as she crossed the lobby to meet the detective leaning against the front desk, a paper cup of coffee from the complimentary service in his hand.

"Thanks for meeting me here," she said. "It's been a busy evening."

Detective Jerry Gadsden had been a friend of their family for years. As she approached, he drew her into a friendly hug. "It's good to see you, though I wish it was purely social. Do you want coffee?"

"No, thank you." She stepped to the open cooler and plucked a bottle of water from the shelf. Her palms were damp, but her throat was dry. She was about to lie to a friend and essentially file a false report.

"Why aren't you at home?" He gestured for her to take a seat on the small sofa, while he settled in the closest chair.

"The gala is tomorrow." She waved a hand in the direction of the wide staircase curving around the atrium and up toward the second level ballrooms. "It's easier to stage the details from here."

He nodded. "You should have waited for the police at the marina."

"I know." Cecelia hesitated. Not because she didn't know how to answer, but because she felt someone watching her. She didn't dare give in to the urge and reveal Emmett's presence. "I was so scared. Those men just burst into the bathroom."

She twisted the cap and took a sip of the water. "Is Heather all right?"

"Heather is the young woman you rescued?"

Cecelia nodded.

"She's shaky, but she'll be fine. Her father said he'd like to thank you."

"I believe he's on the guest list for tomorrow night." Did they think those men had been after Heather? Could she be that lucky?

Detective Gadsden smiled. "You might want to suggest an extra donation for being a hero."

"A hero?" Cecelia laughed that off. "I wouldn't go that far. I only did what any woman would do in my place."

"With great skill, if I might say so."

"You know William insisted on self-defense training for Casey and me."

"Bet you hoped you never had to use it."

She nodded.

"So walk me through what happened."

Cecelia told him the story, minus Emmett's involvement and the previous encounter in the alley.

"Pardon me for saying so, but did you change clothes? Most of the guests at the marina were dressed a bit more for a party than you are now."

She leaned forward, rolled the bottle of water between her palms. "I had a date and we decided to stop by the party on a whim."

"I see."

And she could see the judgment stamped on his face. She wanted to scream but managed a smile, biting back the sharp reminder that it had been over a year since she'd buried her husband. She'd reconciled herself to losing him for more than a year before that. Her counselor had explained that disengaging emotionally was normal under the circumstances. She'd tried to stop it but had failed. William had made her promise she would get on with her life, for heaven's sake.

"How did you meet?"

She sat back, startled by the question. "You can't think my date had anything to do with this?"

"Just gathering information," he said. "We've had an increase in personal thefts. Happens this time of year. And people are more vulnerable to scams during the holidays."

The irony. Emmett was a scammer of an entirely different nature than her friend could comprehend.

"We met online," she said, knowing she had to cooperate. Fighting him would only cast more unwanted suspicion on Emmett. "Three weeks ago."

"Where is he now?" He glanced around the lobby. "I'd like to talk with him."

"You know, I'm not sure." She should have anticipated that question. Her façade was about to crumble. Why did she ever believe she could do this? "I ran out the back and left him there. At the marina. I guess I wasn't such a good date for him. He's probably regretting that expensive dinner he sprang for."

While her friend scrambled to find the proper response, she brushed her bangs off her forehead. "So much for Bachelor Number One." She thought of the kiss, hoping it would make her blush. "I can give you his office number if you'd like to call him tomorrow."

"No home number? No cell?"

She squirmed in her seat. "Guess we hadn't made it to that stage yet. Tonight was our first date in person."

Detective Gadsden picked up on her embarrassment and gave her a sympathetic look. "Dating stinks. When Jen divorced me, it took a while until I felt human again. I know your loss is different, but it will get better."

She appreciated his compassion, and though she should feel bad for misleading him, she didn't. "I'll have to take your word."

"Please do. Now, I still have to give this new friend of yours a call."

"Right." She fished her cell phone out of her purse and read off Emmett's office number.

"Cecelia, do you want me to check him out for you?"

"No. Thank you." She shook her head. "I doubt he'll want to see me again after tonight, anyway."

"If a little random trouble scares him off, he's not good enough for you," Detective Gadsden said.

He had no idea how much she agreed with him. If only she could convince Emmett. "Thanks for the support. Are we done? I'm exhausted."

When he nodded, she stood up, ignoring her wobbling knees. She just wanted to get up to her room before her body collapsed from the post-adrenaline rush.

"You'll be here through the weekend? In case I have other questions," he explained.

"Yes. Tomorrow will go late and it seemed best to crash right here."

"All right." He hugged her again. "Take care of yourself."

"I will."

Detective Gadsden had hardly cleared the lobby before her thoughts turned back to Emmett. She knew he would be close and she made a mental note to ask him where he'd been hiding while she'd talked with the detective. There was no way he'd gone upstairs without her.

He didn't join her in the elevator, and he wasn't waiting in the hallway by her suite door. Worry began to gnaw at her. His absence couldn't be a good thing. She took a step back, ready to go look for him when the door opened.

He filled the doorway with his dark scowl. "What are you waiting for?" He reached out and drew her inside, throwing the deadbolt as soon as the door was closed behind her.

"I thought… Weren't you—"

"I estimated you could make it upstairs on your own."

"Well, of course." She glanced around, noticing a laptop and a garment bag that hadn't been there before she'd left hours ago for the wine bar. His leather jacket was on a hanger in the small closet and he'd stripped off his sweater and rolled back the cuffs of his shirt. She'd never known she could be so attracted to a man's forearms.

She really was in way over her head here. She cleared her throat. "You were serious about sticking *close*."

"Don't worry. I'll bunk on the couch."

"Surely you'd be more comfortable in your own room. I'm safe here." She still had the handgun. A new fear niggled at her. What if the gun had been used to murder someone? She should have mentioned to Gadsden that she'd gotten it from one of those thugs at the marina. Even though that was not quite right, the ones from the alley were likely friends of the two who'd come after her at the marina. But if she'd told him about the gun, he would have wanted to confiscate it. She wasn't ready to turn it over…yet. She might need it.

"And I intend to make sure you stay safe." He used his foot to push the small duffel bag he'd brought from his boat into the space between the chair and sofa. "You told your detective buddy I was protective detail?"

"No. I told him you were my date. A protective detail would have followed me into the lobby." And he knew as well as she did that a protective detail wouldn't have danced with her. Or kissed her senseless.

"A detail might just as easily have kept an eye on you from a distance."

"Which is what you did."

He shrugged.

She changed the subject. "Did you get some ice for your hand?"

"It's fine." He slipped his hands into his pockets. "Get some rest. We can work out a plan for tomorrow in the morning."

She didn't dignify that with a response, too busy studying the contrast his strong, masculine presence made against the filmy tulle of the gift baskets she'd prepared for her planning committee. The entire room was filled to bursting with gala details in a riot of greens, reds and plaids. Folders on the desk were stacked alongside a box of thank-you cards she'd planned to work on after her date. She wasn't up to the task anymore. Two bank boxes of silent auction bid sheets and photos of items too big or too valuable to display were on the counter. Rolls of raffle tickets were stacked next to the boxes. They'd be lucky to find enough space to make coffee in the morning.

The weight of the evening settled heavily onto her. What the hell was she doing? Maybe she'd overestimated her ability. Maybe she was trying to prove something she couldn't manage.

With those daunting thoughts echoing in her head, she fell back on what she knew best. "I should attend to your injuries. Would you like me to brew a cup of coffee?"

"I'm fine, Cecelia. You don't have to be the perfect society hostess here."

If he only knew that she wasn't thinking hostess thoughts at all as she gazed at him. No, her thoughts were sliding down an altogether different path. Maybe she needed the escape. It was the only reasonable explanation for her inability to find her balance in his presence.

When they'd first made plans to meet, she'd indulged in more than a few fantasies of how tonight might go, of what might come next.

She'd never planned to jump straight into bed with him—though he had the body and the face to tempt a saint. But desperate hormones and brotherly warnings aside, she was happy to discover that she had enough self-respect not to be stupid.

She had, however, played out a number of possible good-night scenarios. None of which involved a not-safe-for-work public display of affection on a crowded dance floor. She didn't regret it, other than knowing how much it altered her expectation of any kisses in her future.

Startling and bold as it was, she found herself contemplating how to get him to kiss her again. "Thanks for saving me tonight. I didn't expect the extracurricular, um, fun. I'm glad you were there."

"Just part of the service."

She was immediately irritated by his cavalier attitude until she realized he did it on purpose. He was pushing her away. Unfortunately for him, it only made her more determined to understand why.

"Don't do that," she said, folding her arms over her chest as she faced off with him.

"Do what? We should call it a night. We're both tired."

"Yes, I'm sure we both are. But that's no reason to push away someone who's trying to show a little gratitude."

"You're reading more into this than there is, Cecelia."

"I respectfully disagree." She'd scanned a few of the brief, ambiguous text messages on those phones. As a concerned former wife of an agent and mother of another, she recognized the signs of an agent weary from the task.

"Of course you do." His lip curled in a sneer and he turned his back on her.

If she didn't know better, she'd blame his surly demeanor on the job. But she had experience with others in his field and recognized there was more lurking under the surface.

"Does that loner routine work well for you?"

He spared her an annoyed look as he settled into a chair with his laptop. "Loner would imply that it does."

"I think you're trying to convince yourself you like being alone," she said, falling into the chair next to his. "But the solitude obviously scares you."

"Obviously? What is this, pop-psychology 101?"

Inside, she cringed at the purposely hurtful remark. "Maybe. If you need to talk, I'll listen."

"Talking isn't my preferred form of therapy."

The blatant lust in those enigmatic eyes made her redefine the meaning of attraction. A smart woman would have the sense to run away. She just wanted to get closer. How those cool eyes of his could give off such intense heat was a mystery she wanted to solve. "That was crass."

"But honest."

He had her there. It might have been the most straightforward answer he'd offered. Except it was another answer designed to give him distance. She ought to just honor the signals and retreat, but something, some intangible factor, kept her butt in the chair.

"Emmett—"

He cut her off with a sharp glance. "Enough. I mean it, Cecelia."

She met his steely gaze with one of her own. "Those text messages you had me skim gave a certain impression."

"That we're up against a serious enemy?"

She nearly did a victory dance at the *we* he probably hadn't meant to use.

"That you've basically been a double agent for some time now."

"Which makes me as untrustworthy as your brother believes."

"Not exactly. I got the impression that you're very good at your work."

He stared at her, but his eyes weren't giving her any clues this time.

"You're good enough to make people believe whatever you want them to believe."

He didn't reply.

"What you need them to believe. You just ignore your own needs in the process."

"I still have some research to do." He dropped his head back and spoke to the ceiling. "What will it take to get you to drop this?"

"One answer. Do you really enjoy photography?"

He rolled his head toward her, his lips parted

on an unspoken oath and a "how is that relevant" look in his eyes.

She arched an eyebrow, waiting.

"Yes," he replied quietly. "Now go on and get some rest. You've got a big day tomorrow."

She left him alone to do his research. After going through her nightly rituals, Cecelia slipped between the sheets of the big hotel bed and stared at the ceiling. Her racing thoughts kept circling back to one place: her brother and daughter might be right after all. If her shaking hands were any indication, she wasn't cut out for ops.

She laced her fingers and tried a slow, meditative breath. It didn't help. She was too frustrated with the way she'd barely managed to carry on with a date and keep her senses about her. Granted, the date had been complicated by other issues, but so would her life be if—*when*—she made the career change.

Logically, she knew training would prepare her, give her the tools to carry out fieldwork more effectively. Still, her hands rattled against the cool, smooth sheets.

Her first date since losing her husband and she had nearly got the man killed in an alley brawl because she wouldn't give up her purse. Thomas had been right to doubt her when she'd volunteered to be an asset. She'd only been fooling herself to believe she could do this.

She closed her eyes and saw that broken bottle slice through the air toward Emmett. One false move and he would have been the one needing a paramedic.

She was exaggerating. It was a lesson in perspective. The moment only looked worse to her because she'd been scared. But Emmett had held his own. More than that. He'd been so calm, so professional.

Rolling to her side, she punched and fluffed the pillow. She'd had more training than the average woman, knew better than most people how to protect herself in a physical altercation. William had insisted on teaching her what he thought she needed to know in case she'd ever been targeted by *his* enemies.

Yet, tonight, when it had mattered, she'd pulled out the Taser at the first opportunity. So much for her bold eagerness to jump into fieldwork.

She closed her eyes and tried to see her husband's face, tried to imagine what he would have said or done if he'd been in that alley with her. The image was more difficult to conjure than it should have been.

Instead, Emmett dodging the broken bottle, landing uppercuts and that jaw-cracking hook, those were the images that filled her mind. The more she tried and failed, the worse she felt about the whole evening.

What kind of loving wife gave a man two and a half decades, nursed him through a terminal illness and then blanked him from her mind when the first bit of eye candy showed an interest?

A false interest, she added, factoring in the rest of the details.

She told herself this exercise would be easier if she'd been at home. In the back of her bureau drawer, she kept one of William's favorite T-shirts. All of his other clothes had been donated to charity, but that shirt was her last indulgence, a sachet of memories when she buried her nose deep in search of his scent.

A scent that had faded months ago.

Live your life.

At the time, she'd smiled and promised to do just that, knowing he was already more than halfway gone. She'd been by his side through every terrible stage of his disease, but shutting down her emotions had been the only way to survive the agony of watching his body wage war against the unrelenting cancer.

His doctors and nurses had told her to put him in hospice, but she couldn't justify it. She'd been strong enough to care for him, and her employer had held her job while she'd done what needed to be done.

Though he was too ill to know in his last weeks, she'd honored his last wish. He'd died peacefully in his own home, surrounded by the familiar things they'd collected in the process of building their life as husband and wife.

By the time his body had surrendered, her relief was palpable. She barely had tears left to shed at the memorial as so much of her grieving had been done in those quiet, endless hours alone with him.

Friends and family called her brave. She didn't have the courage to correct them. Didn't have the decency to admit she'd parked her heart back with that last good conversation and simply gone through the motions until his struggle had finally ended.

Tonight had proved she hadn't gained any courage in the year since. She'd let Emmett handle everything while she'd mostly cowered.

William would agree with Casey and Thomas and tell her she had no business in ops. As much as she wanted to reinvent her life, herself, maybe she should stick with the more passive pursuits of charity fundraising and…needlepoint.

She groaned into the pillow. She'd always hated needlepoint.

"Cecelia?"

He was silhouetted in the bedroom doorway, the light from the other room glowing behind him. "I'm fine," she said in a rush. "Didn't mean to wake you."

She was half tempted to send her brother a text

and let him know she'd basically wound up in protective custody after all. Of course, Thomas probably still considered Emmett the enemy.

She couldn't believe she was sharing a room with a man again. In the broadest sense of the word, anyway. Who knew a year could make so much difference? It had been even longer than that since she'd had a healthy partner to share any part of her life with, and she'd learned to rely on herself. The challenges had taught her she enjoyed quiet, setting her own schedule and having no one to answer to.

But that left no one to answer her.

The silhouette shifted. "Need to talk about it?"

"No, thank you," she replied.

"Now who's ignoring their needs?"

"I'm fine," she said firmly.

"You did well tonight."

She didn't have a polite reply for that. It seemed rude to argue with the man who'd saved her from being kidnapped. Twice. The man who refused to leave her alone in the hotel suite she'd booked for the weekend just to simplify logistics for tomorrow's event.

Admin and logistics, those were her strengths, a little voice reminded her. Not ops.

"Do I make you uncomfortable?"

Yes! "No," she said. Both answers were true,

but she couldn't possibly explain that to him. She rolled onto her back and sat up, uncaring if her hair was tousled. "Are you uncomfortable here with me?"

There was a long pause before he said, "I'm worried about you."

He didn't strike her as the worrying type. "Why?"

"Anyone would be in shock after what we handled tonight."

"You can rest easy. I'm not in shock."

Racked with guilt about forgetting my husband so easily, yes. Shock, not so much. Between her family and her job—even as an admin for the CIA—she'd heard enough to know what had happened could have been much worse.

The silhouette at the door moved again. *Come closer,* she pleaded silently. *Touch me, talk to me. Help me forget what a horrible person I am.* But using him that way would only compound her mistakes. As much as she wanted a repeat performance of that kiss on the dance floor, she'd had enough guilt for one day.

She'd used those unending hours during the long, lonely months to think about what being a widow meant to her, what her life would look like without a husband to provide and care for. In her mind she'd seen herself growing stronger with her forced independence. Now she wondered what kind of fantasy she'd been spinning.

"All right. I'm a light sleeper if you change your mind."

She was a light sleeper, too. First as a result of motherhood, and more recently from all those nights listening for her husband's final breath. Emotions tangled inside her, threatened to burst from her. "Emmett, wait."

"Yes?"

"Tomorrow." She fisted her fingers in the sheet. "Will you please show me how you got the information off the phones?"

"You want a technology lesson?"

"If you don't mind."

"Sure. Nothing I did tonight is a big secret."

"Can I help you research the Irina name?"

"That's what I've been doing. It's a yacht registered in the Bahamas."

"Oh."

"The text could just as easily reference a new associate. We can dig deeper tomorrow."

She sensed he was holding something back. "Okay. When it's time, will you really let me help?"

"Time?"

"When you're ready to wrap this up, I mean."

"Are you asking to help me plan and execute the takedown?"

She swallowed. "I'm already scheduled to be the bait, aren't I?"

He moved through the darkness of the room toward her. The dim light from the door backlit him, but she couldn't see his face or his eyes. His scent filled her senses and she felt the mattress sag as he sat on the corner of the bed.

"No matter what your brother said, I won't let anyone hurt you. That was never the plan."

"I believe you." She scooted closer to him, to his heat. Maybe she had lost her mind but she just couldn't help herself. "Let me help you. At least show me how not to be a stumbling block and what you're planning."

"You have the gala and your guests to think about."

"Gracious hostess is a role I've mastered. Could do it blindfolded. What you could teach me will help me when I move to ops."

"We don't exactly do things according to CIA protocol, Cecelia."

She wanted to reach for the light so she could gauge his expression but knew it would blow the intimacy of the moment and snap the fragile thread of hope that he might agree. "It would still be an informative exercise."

He huffed a derisive breath. "Too informative is more like it. What I've been doing has been dark since I learned Isely was gunning for Thomas and everything he's built at Mission Recovery."

"Teach me or I won't go quietly when it's time to take me to Isely."

"Blackmail doesn't suit you." The bed shifted as Emmett stood up. "You have no idea what you're asking." His silhouette filled the doorway again. "Get some sleep and we'll discuss it in the morning."

It wasn't the yes she'd hoped for, but it wasn't an outright no. Cecelia pulled the covers close, a smile on her face as she settled her head on the pillow. After a moment, she realized her hands weren't shaking anymore.

Maybe there was hope for her, after all.

Chapter Ten

Holt's phone rang at five minutes past eight o'clock. Nice of the detective to give him time to settle at the desk job indicated by his profile at the online dating site. Why couldn't she have just stuck with the protective custody idea? Her detective pal would have bought that line considering who her husband had been.

The questions were easy enough that he might have handled them in his sleep, which was a good thing considering his mind was otherwise occupied with thoughts of the woman in the bedroom.

She didn't seem to have any idea at the wealth of talent lurking inside her. She'd played the detective brilliantly last night. If he hadn't already known it from watching the interview, the tone of the detective's questions today would have confirmed it.

"I suggest you move on to the next woman on your list," Detective Gadsden said.

Holt was amused by the detective's lack of subtlety. "Do you have a vested interest in Mrs. Manning?" He hoped not. He had enough—more than enough—adversaries to dodge on this op already.

"I've known her a long time. She deserves better than a man who'd leave her stranded."

"Check your notes, detective. She ran out on me." He disconnected the call and pushed the phone onto the clip on his hip.

He returned to his computer and considered checking in with Nadine, or even the director, but changed his mind. Neither of them could tell him what he wanted to know: Why was Isely rushing the plan?

He thought back to the intel on that flash drive. He'd precisely crafted the files he'd given to Isely, embellishing where necessary to blur the truth. It was his fault Isely knew about Cecelia, and whether the director ever believed him or not, he'd guarded her carefully since he'd been forced to reveal the connection.

He'd assumed kidnapping Cecelia was simply one part of Isely's plan for the director's downfall. But the shift, the new desperation, didn't fit and it brought up a host of potential disasters.

There had only been two changes in Cecelia's life since Isely proposed this kidnapping. Her online relationship and her internal career change within the CIA.

Holt didn't like the way it was adding up. According to her, she didn't do anything all that interesting in her little corner of administration. He scrubbed at his face. As much as he dreaded it, he was going to have to interrogate Cecelia about her work.

"Everything okay?" Cecelia asked from the doorway.

"Fine. Just dealt with your detective." He turned to face her and wished he hadn't. She'd emerged from the bedroom with a well-rested glow. Bright green lace peeked out from the white of the fluffy hotel robe she wore. "Coffee's ready."

"Thanks." She crossed the room, wisely giving him a wide berth, and poured herself a cup. "So what's first?"

"Breakfast."

By the time they'd pushed the room-service cart back into the hallway and she'd left to take a shower, the implied intimacy was getting under his skin.

He hadn't lived in such close proximity to a woman since the dorms in college. The scents and sounds and rituals had been intriguing, amusing and thoroughly educational on a less-than-academic level.

After two failed attempts at real relationships,

he had given up on the idea of a true and lasting one in favor of hot, brief affairs where both parties knew what they were getting into.

You lied to me. Her words echoed in his mind this morning every time he looked at her. Lying was part of his life, and his secrets had been the breaking point of those early relationships. As a Specialist, the need for deception hadn't changed. Not with this case, and not with her.

He was more than a little surprised Director Casey hadn't kicked down the door yet to protect both his sister and the team he was sure Holt was deceiving. By now the man had to know they were together. Or had been together. Well, not together-together, though that still held serious appeal.

He pushed a hand through his hair and forced himself to stop overthinking the situation with Cecelia.

She was a means to an end. He had measures in place so she'd never really be in jeopardy. Unfortunately, he couldn't explain that to anyone yet. Not even her. Only sincere worry and a convincing effort by Thomas to rescue her would convince Isely of his loyalty.

He heard the hair dryer start up and knew he only had a few minutes more to think up something else to teach her. She'd mastered the phone dumps over the scrambled eggs. He understood what she was really asking and he gave her points for turning what might have been an awkward situation to her favor.

She'd warned him their day would be consistently interrupted with her friends calling and even coming and going from the suite. To prevent questions, they'd moved all of his belongings into the bedroom.

If anyone caught them together before the gala, she promised to refer to him as her security detail. He figured it was too little too late, especially after that kiss on the dance floor last night. No doubt someone at the party had captured the moment with a camera or cell phone. He'd been more than a little surprised the detective hadn't come across it yet.

He was rubbing his lips, remembering the moment, when a soft rap on the door drew his attention. He crossed the room, peered through the peephole and saw two brunettes in the stylish conservative attire that marked all of her friends. He felt underdressed in the faded jeans and black polo shirt he'd pulled on after his shower, but he opened the door anyway.

"Oh." The bright smiles faded as both women gaped at him. "We must, ah…"

"Looking for Cecelia?"

"Yes," they replied in unison, obviously relieved and startled at the same time.

"Names?"

They frowned, but gave him the information. Recognizing the names from the list of expected visitors Cecelia had given him, he stepped back and invited them inside.

"I'm with hotel security," he lied. "I'll let her know you're here."

He walked away before they could ask him why she needed security in her room, but his excellent hearing caught the murmurs of appreciation and speculation that he was the same guy spotted with Cecelia last night.

Great.

Last night's stunt at the marina had clearly made Cecelia grist for the gossip mill. It was all he could do not to remind these two they were supposed to be her friends.

He kept his mouth shut. If Cecelia moved into ops, she'd have to deal with twisted perceptions as a natural part of getting through the day.

Holt paused at the bathroom door, his train of thought completely derailed at the sight of Cecelia wrapped only a bath towel.

Other women he'd spent time with in close proximity had done their hair last. Not her.

Catching his reflection in the mirror, she turned off the hair dryer. "Problem?"

His temper flared in an automatic defense against the rush of lust coursing through his body. "There's a perfectly good robe right here," he growled, pulling it off the hook and tossing it at her. "You've got company."

She smiled at him, her polite "life is lovely" smile. "I'll be right out."

He turned, uncertain of how to escape. He didn't want to chat with the Junior League twins in the other room and he couldn't stand here staring as Cecelia put on something more appropriate.

He bit back an oath and crossed to the window in the bedroom, positioning himself so she had privacy. Maybe he'd get lucky and a sniper would put him out of his misery.

The suite door opened and closed, the feminine voices rose and fell and then Cecelia returned to the bedroom. He didn't have to look—the light floral scent of her body wash drifted across the room and teased his senses.

"You can turn around. I'm dressed and they're gone."

He turned, but it was a mistake. The cream colored, body-skimming top with spaghetti-thin straps and jeans that molded to her hips and thighs were almost more tempting than the towel had been.

A vivid image of him sliding those straps down and away played out in his head before he yanked his gaze back up to her eyes. "We have work to do."

"I'm ready." She pulled on a thick cardigan

sweater and walked back out to the sitting room. He enjoyed the sweet view of her backside, then had to wait a moment until he was sure he had his wayward lust under control.

He couldn't let this attraction interfere with what had to be done here.

As he joined her in the other room she announced, "We have an hour or so before Casey stops by."

"Awesome." He picked up his laptop and set it on the low coffee table in front of the couch. "Isely wanted to kidnap you last night," he began without preamble. "We need to dig in and find out why he changed his schedule."

"Changed?"

"Yeah. The original plan was to take you from the gala tonight. Bigger shock value," he pointed out.

"So should I assume he'll make another attempt?"

"Yes."

"Okay." She picked up her tablet. "What do you want me to do?"

"When they grab you, don't panic."

She tilted her head, laced her fingers and pushed her hands forward like a pianist limbering up before a recital. "Okay. I meant what do you want me to do now? Can I research the location in that text message?"

"Go ahead." Inspiration struck. "See if you can connect the location to the name of the ship."

"If the yacht is the Irina we're after."

"Exactly."

Reluctantly, he sat beside her and started his own search for the possible catalysts that might have Isely looking at Cecelia.

After a few comfortable minutes of silence, she said, "I think we're after the yacht. Those numbers come up as a location in the Atlantic Ocean, not too far off the coast."

Holt mentally cringed. That kind of "address" didn't bode well for Cecelia or Thomas's chances of rescuing her. Isely knew Holt could sail, and an exchange at sea likely meant Isely had found Holt's boat in the marina.

Not good. Even worse was that the location hadn't been sent to Holt, only to one of Isely's most trusted men. Holt started searching slip registrations for rentals matching the original operation timeline.

"Are you hacking into the marina?" Cecelia was looking over his shoulder. "You promised to show me your process."

Not exactly, but there was no use getting into a debate. "If he means to sail into the sunset with you, we need to be prepared."

"Do you like working with my brother?"

The question came out of nowhere. She was

constantly surprising him with her accurate assessments, even when her mind seemed to be elsewhere. Director Casey was the kind of boss who had a man's back. It was the one piece of this task that regularly pricked at Holt's conscience. Thomas Casey didn't see eye to eye with Holt, and that was never going to change. This mission would be the final straw for Holt. Win or lose— and Mission Recovery would win—he'd started to realize no one would ever trust him again.

Even if he came away from this clean, without that trust he could never take over for Director Casey as planned. He'd known this was a career-ending op but hadn't bothered to dwell on it. Had in fact been in active denial about it as recently as yesterday when he'd tasked Grant with finding the biologist.

"Emmett?"

"Your brother is a good man and a good boss. I've got nothing but respect for him."

"You're doing this—and planning to take the fall—to protect him."

He turned on her to let her see the dark edges he hid behind layers of polish and training. "I'm doing this because it needs to be done. Isely has a deadly new bioweapon and he blames your brother for the death of his father and undermining their business reputation. I'm doing what I have to do."

"He certainly seems to be paying plenty of people to come after me."

"That's what bothers me," Holt admitted. "The original plan was simple. Just me, you and a drop-off point."

"Hmm."

He didn't like the sound of that hmm. He tried to ignore it, to finish the trail of breadcrumbs that would help Director Casey save Cecelia in case things went sideways on him tonight.

"What?"

"Nothing. Just wondering what you made him believe about you."

He sighed, closed the top on his computer. "Why do you care?"

"You promised to teach me something. How did you convince him you could be bought?"

"Why do you think it's as simple as money?"

"Because you donated a substantial amount of money to my charity. I suspect that was because you didn't want any part of the money he had paid you."

He stood up and paced away from her. "Nothing better to dump it into."

"Maybe not, but I think it's more likely you enjoyed putting his blood money to good use."

How in the hell did she see him so clearly? "The donation put me in your circle." He waved his hands to indicate the suite. "What better way to enable Isely's vengeance?"

"Hmm."

"Stop that," he snapped.

"What?" She gave an exaggerated flutter of her eyelashes.

"Isely has to believe you're oblivious." He'd convinced jaded, field-tested operatives on both sides of the law, but he couldn't fool this one woman. "Lives are on the line here, Cecelia."

"I understand." She set aside her tablet and walked straight up to him. "More than you, I think."

Nothing short of a major earthquake could have uprooted him as she wrapped him in a hug. A *hug,* for crying out loud. He didn't know where to put his hands, so he kept them off her.

"Thank you," she said, "for everything you've sacrificed to protect Thomas." Her heart was shining in her eyes as she gazed up at him. "Casey's wedding day would have been ruined without Thomas."

"He got himself out of that. I had nothing to do with it."

With one last squeeze, she stepped back, and her lips curved into a warm, sincere smile. "I don't believe you."

"It's the truth." He rubbed at his mouth, told himself to shut up. "I'm not the white knight from a fairy tale." But she made him want to be, and he hated himself for the failure.

The thought was so foreign, so unprecedented, he actually didn't know what to say next.

She slid into the chair, crossed her legs and drummed her fingers against the upholstery. "Oh, no, you're definitely bad-guy material. At least that's what you want me to believe."

"It's more true than you know."

"If you say so." She shrugged one delicate shoulder and blew him off.

"God, you're stubborn."

"I am. It comes in handy." She reached over and patted the couch. "Now, come on and show me something useful before we get interrupted again. I'm not letting you renege."

"A bad guy would renege," he pointed out.

"I'm sure you're right."

She was going into ops, and from what he'd heard through the bugs he'd planted in her house, no one close to her supported the decision.

Sure, they'd had more years with her, knew her far better than he did. Apparently that blurred their vision, or maybe they just didn't realize how strong she had to be to do what she'd been doing all these years: waiting and praying that a loved one in harm's way would come home safe.

From where he stood, Cecelia Manning was smart, brave and determined. Possibly too determined, he amended as she continued to stare him down. The CIA would be lucky to have her in an operations capacity.

He pulled up one of the fake files he'd given Isely and a picture he'd previously sent to use as an example. Side by side from his laptop to hers, he taught her the basics of how he manipulated the intel. She was a quick study, using the tips he showed her to embed information in photographs, to transfer files away from the home system and to leave breadcrumbs that pointed in another direction.

"Emmett?" She waited for him to glance at her screen. "How does this look?" She tucked her hands under her legs as if she feared he would see them tremble as he reviewed her first effort at concealing information in a digital photo.

He reviewed her coding, then asked her to show him the research she'd found on the Irina. "Thomas is an idiot."

CECELIA'S FINGERS WENT still on the keyboard. As a little sister perpetually in her brother's shadow, it wasn't that she didn't have cause to agree, but she wanted to be sure why this man thought so. "Do I need to defend my brother?"

"I bugged your house, remember? I heard that crack he made about not recruiting you."

"Familiarity breeds contempt," she said lightly.

She'd had a lifetime to get used to it. "It would be more accurate to say he's averse to change. I'm the baby sister and I've been a predictable and known quantity in his life since I was born. He can't help wanting to keep me in that box."

"I have a feeling your current situation will blow the lid right off that box," he said.

"Agreed." She switched to another window so he could check that code, as well. "Did I do this one right?"

"Nice work."

She wanted to celebrate but decided to save it for private. "Thanks."

"You'll make a good partner one day."

"Not that you ever use them."

"What do you mean?"

"I was thinking of last night and the possible break-in at my house. You were with me, and you appear to be working this operation alone. Or you were. Who else would have cause to search my home?"

His cool eyes went flat and she knew he shared her concern. "I've wanted to ask you about that and about your work. It's possible Isely thinks you know something or can access something valuable."

"I don't know anything of value to a man like him. Unless he's in the market for a human-resources lackey."

"You're no lackey," he grumbled.

She appreciated the vote of confidence, especially from this unexpected source. "I'll do a little research—"

"No. Leave that to me. I have more free time than you do today."

She glanced at her watch. "Casey and the girls will be here soon. We have appointments with the hotel spa before it's time to dress for the evening."

"Tell me I don't have to go along."

His stricken expression made her laugh. "Relax, no one's going to tie you down and force you to have a mani-pedi."

"I don't want to know what that is."

"Such a bachelor," she teased.

"Always." He packed up his computer. "If you promise not to leave the hotel, there are a few things I should see to in person."

"Isely?"

"Best to keep a volatile client calm."

As if he read her worry before she could say a word, he traced the curve of her shoulder with his fingertip, instantly distracting her. "I'll come back up to dress when you've all cleared out."

"But you will be there tonight?" The thought of never seeing him again slashed through her, made her ache.

He nodded.

"Say the words, Emmett. Tell me you'll be at

the gala as my guest, not just because Isely wants you to be there." She hadn't meant to say that last part, but there it was.

"I'll be there for you."

"Thank you," she whispered, weak with relief.

A new awareness arced between them. For her it came from having an expert field agent take her seriously as much as her growing affection for a man determined to stand apart from the world... and to keep her safe in the process.

He wasn't the only one who knew his way around and through computer systems. At his side, she'd done almost as much digging as learning today, and discovered his past—at least those days before he went behind the technological curtain of Mission Recovery—was full of white-knight behavior.

Since June he'd systematically alienated each of his allies, but thanks to what he'd taught her, she knew he was doing all the wrong things for all the right reasons.

She understood she might very well be interpreting his actions favorably on purpose, but she didn't care. Intuition told her that white knight had been buried deep, for a long time, as a matter of survival.

"Give me your phone."

She found it on the table and handed it to him. He entered something and handed it back. "Keep it on and keep it with you. As long as Casey stays close, he won't make a move. I'm speed-dial one if anything happens. Just call and leave the line open."

"And if you need me?"

His smile sent butterflies winging through her belly. "You'll know."

"Emmett, whatever happens tonight, please know that I trust you."

He stared at her for a long moment. "Sweetheart, you really shouldn't."

Chapter Eleven

She had to admire his timing. Emmett had cleared the suite minutes before Casey had knocked on the door. They caught up on family and simple things, but serious talk had to wait as her friends arrived to help shuttle things downstairs.

They'd just returned from setting up the gift table when the suite phone rang and Cecelia cringed as Casey picked it up. What if it was Emmett? Would her daughter disapprove of her social life as much as she disapproved of her new career goals? Would she call Thomas and give away Emmett's location?

"Sure, she's right here." Casey covered the receiver with her palm. "A detective for you."

"Jerry?"

Casey shook her head as Cecelia took the phone and introduced herself.

"Ah, Mrs. Manning. If you could come down to the hotel café, please. We just need another moment of your time."

"We're terribly busy. I gave my statement to Detective Gadsden last night. Can't this wait until tomorrow?"

"I'm afraid not. We have suspects in holding, but I can't keep them there without cause. I just need you to take a look at a few photos."

"Of course. I'll be right down."

She knew there was more to it. Detective Gadsden should have been asking her these questions. The voice wasn't quite right, either, but she refused to cower again. She'd be safe enough in the café with her daughter beside her.

"I have to go downstairs for a moment and look at a couple of pictures. Apparently they have some suspects in last night's trouble. Will you come with me?"

"Sure, Mom."

Cecelia gave an excuse to the other women who were taking the last load of items out of the suite, then she and Casey headed downstairs.

"It didn't sound like Detective Gadsden," Casey said.

"No, it wasn't. He must have sent a colleague." She punched the button for the lobby level as well as the floor above it. "Can you keep an eye on me—be my backup—and still let me handle whatever this is?"

"Are you expecting trouble?"

"After last night, I wouldn't be surprised by

anything." That was an understatement, for sure. "It should be a straightforward process, but if I'm wrong, do the right thing and call your uncle."

"You know I will."

Cecelia's palms were damp as the elevator stopped and the doors opened at the second floor. "I mean it, honey. Don't interfere, just make the call."

Casey didn't look happy about it, but she made the promise as the doors closed between them.

At the café, a man with dark hair brushed back from a face that might have passed for mid-twenties stood up from a nearby table as she paused at the hostess station.

"Mrs. Manning?" He flashed a badge, and then extended his hand. "A pleasure to meet you. I've ordered coffee."

Closer now, she could see he wasn't as young as first glance implied. "Thank you, but I'm terribly short on time."

"A big night ahead of you." He gestured for her to join him at his table.

"Yes." She settled into a chair and waited for him to resume his.

"I've heard about the gala. The pediatric department is fortunate you're on their side."

He was a little too slick for Cecelia's taste, and there was something in his eyes that warned her to tread carefully. Her phone was in her lap, turned on and ready to press the number one.

"It was my husband's idea, and I'm pleased to carry it out." She poured herself a cup of coffee in hopes of appearing far calmer than she was.

He pushed a folder across the table and opened it. Only two pictures were inside, and neither of them bore the slightest resemblance to last night's assailants. She looked from a candid shot of her brother to a similarly candid shot of Emmett. Then she looked back up at the man who was certainly not a detective.

And then she knew. She'd walked right into his trap. "Mr. Isely?"

He nodded. "Forgive the deception."

Emmett would be furious, and she'd never forgive her stupidity if she let herself get taken. She scooted her chair away from the table. "I really must get back to the preparations upstairs."

"But I only need a moment. Which man means more to you, I wonder?"

Terror lit in her body. The air in her lungs turned to stone.

"Do give me an answer. I have a man positioned behind your daughter, ready to put a bullet in her head at my command."

With a steady hand, Cecelia raised her coffee cup to her lips, smiling over the rim. She would not alarm the other patrons or give this monster any reason to hurt her daughter.

"I love my brother."

"Blood over lust, then?"

She waited, her hands calm in her lap as she glanced around. "Where is Mr. Holt?"

"Not to worry, he'll be here to dance with you again tonight. As they say, I'm banking on it."

Who was this man? He dared to make a move like this—in the open? He had to know that her brother as well as Emmett would be watching her. The bastard seemed fearless. *Do this right, Cecelia.* She needed to play the part. Make the right moves. For all their sakes. "Will you be in attendance, as well? I might be able to arrange a seat in exchange for an appropriate donation."

Isely stared at her. "You are remarkable."

"Thank you." She set the cup down, thankfully without cracking the saucer. "If you'll excuse me?"

"Not quite yet. Where is the formula?"

"I have no idea what you're talking about." And that lack of knowledge sent a chill skating down her spine. This man was dangerous in a way she'd never faced before. She'd met all kinds of people through her husband's career and living in this area, and she knew everyone had secrets. But Isely oozed lethal in an entirely different capacity.

"You are a very poor liar," he said. "I advise you to choose discretion over valor here, Mrs. Manning. Unless your skills improve, you will need a great deal of assistance from friends in your new career. We might come to a mutually profitable arrangement if you cooperate now."

"I believe the term is 'asset.' And I will never be one of yours."

"Tell me where I can find the formula or I will take down your brother and expose his crimes for the world to judge."

His threats and arrogance ignited something dark and deadly deep inside her. She felt the shift like an earthquake as her resolve kicked into high gear. She never considered herself capable of blood lust, but she had an overwhelming need to send Mr. Isely straight to hell. The man sold weapons to the highest bidder, invested in research for the sole purpose of profiting from atrocities. He was as low as a life form could be.

"You'll try to do that anyway," she countered.

"Try?" He arched a brow. "No, no. I always succeed in my endeavors. However, one detail from you could prevent much suffering."

"No. I don't quite trust you, sir." She knew he would eventually try to take down Thomas anyway, for the sake of his revenge if he got nothing else from this venture. She had to pause to keep from shouting. Or leaping across the table and attempting to strangle him. Either action would surely be construed as a signal to shoot Casey. "As for Thomas, he can take care of himself."

"I know you need to believe it."

It was too much. He didn't know her, would never know her. The pricey suit and cultured voice were merely a costume to hide his lack of humanity. By design or circumstance, he'd become something absolutely vile. But he would never know her or her brother.

"You know nothing about me or my needs." She was a moment away from tossing the coffeepot at his head. "I cannot give you what I do not have. I suggest you take your own advice and discreetly crawl back under the rock where you belong."

"Well, well." He sat back in his chair, a reptilian smile sliding across his face. "You are a delightful surprise. I am so honored, Mrs. Manning, to be the first to see this side of you."

"You will not succeed." She leaned forward. "I won't let you."

"Oh, I look forward to our next meeting." He stood. She did the same. "Have a lovely evening."

She had to find Emmett… She blinked, realized she had totally forgotten to hit the speed dial for him.

Too late to worry about that now. She had to find her daughter.

Chapter Twelve

Plaza Hotel, 7:35 p.m.

From across the balcony, Holt watched Cecelia navigate the sparkling rainbow of expensive gowns anchored by tailored and rented tuxedos. Most of the men had worn classic black tie, but a few had chosen more festive touches of holiday color in honor of the season.

Holt wasn't one of them. He'd been honest with her about that. He didn't do holidays, had never had a reason to. In her red tulle ball gown with its jeweled waist she was as untouchable as ever; still, his hands itched to do so.

He only had to keep himself under control for one more night. Then it would be over, one way or another.

With a flute of champagne in his hand, he exchanged pleasantries with people who only assumed they knew him, and wondered if he'd been foolish to attempt this alone. Cecelia had been right about one thing. He was exhausted from maintaining surveillance to assure her safety, searching her history for common ground and keeping up appearances at his real job. It would all be worth it if he could get her out of here alive and stop Isely.

The large crowd, even bigger than he'd expected, shifted and flexed, blocking his view of her again. He hustled up the staircase to take a better position. There was a younger blonde glued to her side. The daughter. At least Cecelia was guarded well. Even without the benefit of the research photos he'd studied, their resemblance was uncanny. And while he hadn't spotted Director Casey specifically, Holt knew he'd have several people in place.

Now he just had to dance between the sharp blades of Isely's revenge and the director's protective nature. Preferably without getting sliced to ribbons in the process.

Since Isely's first warning, Holt had searched through every detail about Cecelia's life. Nothing he'd turned up indicated any reason to worry about her endangering Isely's ultimate revenge plot against Thomas.

Today, as he'd put his escape plan and backup options in place, he dug deeper still and hadn't found the thing that explained Isely's uncharacteristic impatience. He'd searched headlines and found no change in current events. He'd poured through obituary columns and death notices and come up empty.

The widow had no field experience, and though the CIA employed her, it was in a legitimate, low-key administration post. She'd only recently returned to that post after taking four months' leave to care for her husband during his losing battle with brain cancer.

She hadn't been close enough to the agency to even catch a rumor that might assist or harm the German crime lord, and yet Holt couldn't shake the feeling that something was very, very wrong.

What did Isely know about the woman that had him so focused on her?

It remained the unanswered question, so Holt turned his mind to what he did know: Isely. The man was smart. Devious. Determined beyond reason to destroy Thomas Casey. As the sister, Cecelia had obvious value as leverage to cause pain. People were mere tools to a man like him.

Thank God there weren't too many men like Isely in the world. Of course, in Holt's line of work he saw more than his fair share of them.

A man with a booming voice announced the orchestra was ready, and three wide ballroom doors opened on cue.

He watched the crowd flow through them, Cecelia and her daughter standing at the center greeting donors with gracious smiles. Other people important to the charity foundation did the same at the other two doors, but Holt decided he'd wasted enough time.

Setting his champagne aside, he returned to the ballroom level and gave Casey a cursory nod as he greeted Cecelia. Immediately the daughter went on alert, but Cecelia's perfect society smile didn't so much as flicker.

He didn't know whether he should be pleased or insulted.

"So glad you've arrived, Mr. Holt," she said. With a quiet word to her daughter, she slipped her arm through his. "Let me show you to your table."

This was unexpected. "That's really not necessary. I just wanted you to know I was here."

"I knew." Her smile remained, but her blue eyes showed clear relief.

"What happened?" He'd had his phone on all day. His random yet frequent checks of her safety had indicated nothing untoward had occurred. "You didn't call."

"There was no need. This way."

She guided him through the sea of round tables set for ten and he took stock of the setup, comparing the final arrangement to the plans he'd read in her suite last night. At the far end of the room, on the other side of the wide dance floor, the long head table perched on a riser. A podium stood ready at the center of the head table, a small orchestra to one side and what appeared to be a DJ's table on the other.

Two walls of the ballroom were lined with long tables draped in snow-white linen and decorated with Christmas colors. Silent auction items were laid out with suggested starting bids on each paper. Four bar stations were prepped, but currently closed.

His concern grew with every step she took closer to that head table. He'd known his donation would get her attention, but being front and center was more publicity than he wanted. Dining with half of the moneyed elite of Alexandria and Washington, D.C., wasn't his idea of discreet. Would nothing go right in this last stage of his plans?

Alarms went off in his head when a familiar couple entered through a side door. Lucas Camp and his wife, Victoria Colby-Camp, strolled in, Lucas's limp barely evident this evening. They approached the round table closest to the dance floor and were soon joined by Thomas Casey and Cecelia's daughter, along with her husband, Levi.

He'd known about the connection. Cecelia considered Camp a dear friend. The man was Casey's godfather. But of all the friends she might have in attendance, this one man, working with or without Thomas, could ruin everything.

It was increasingly clear Holt was going down in flames tonight. He'd been prepared for that. But he could not let any of them get in the way of his keeping Cecelia safe.

Still, of all the contingency plans he'd made, this was one he hadn't anticipated. He started crafting an excuse to leave, knowing he could duck back in and take her later, but she led him straight up to a place at the end of the head table. Next to a place card with her name.

What the hell?

As the event organizer, shouldn't she be closer to the podium? Relieved as he was not to be seated with Camp, he had to wonder what game she was playing.

"This isn't necessary."

"Of course it is," she countered. "You single-handedly lifted us to our pre-event goal and your gift will inspire others in the room to follow your example and give generously."

"I can't."

"You must." She lowered her voice, but there would be no argument. "Anything less would be an insult." She squeezed his arm. "Stop scowling. Besides, I need you."

That declaration hadn't been easy for her. He nodded. Something had rattled her today and she wanted him to help her cope. Why hadn't she called him? As often as he'd checked in on her, how the hell had anything significant happened? Wouldn't her daughter have sounded an alert? Casey had been with her mother the entirety of the day.

The way Cecelia looked at him, waiting for his answer, a surge of protectiveness shot through him, and he patted her hand, warming her cold fingers. "I'm here."

"Thank you." She nodded toward others finding seats at the other end of the long table. "Let me introduce you."

"I look forward to it," he lied with an easy smile.

He could feel Camp's eyes boring into his back and the urge to turn around or roll his shoulders was overwhelming. He resisted, thanks to the years of practice at controlling or denying his physical responses for the sake of the job at hand.

Bring on the overcooked chicken and speeches so he could retreat, he thought. With her. His instincts were prickling and he kept an eye on the shadows for any sign of Isely's thugs or Thomas's Specialists.

He supposed he should add Colby's agents to the list of possible party crashers. Unfortunately, he hadn't done his homework on them.

Well, there were worse things than winging it, and as soon as he had her out of this hotel, he'd have the advantage once more.

CECELIA HAD BEEN more than a little relieved when Emmett had finally joined her at the door. She'd worried all day that somehow Isely had uncovered his betrayal and taken action.

Keeping the unexpected encounter with Isely to herself had been the right thing to do. That monster intended not only to destroy Thomas but also to destroy Emmett. She had to stop him. Neither her brother nor the man beside her would want her to act on her own instincts. After all, she had no real training to speak of. But she suspected that was the only way to help both of them.

She had to do this. Yet she was no fool. Her daughter had her back. Cecelia was reasonably sure she had half convinced Casey that Emmett really was trying to protect her.

He was far closer to being that white knight than he realized.

She'd known the moment he'd joined the cocktail reception. Something in the air changed when he was near, when she felt his gaze on her. It was a sensation she'd never thought to experience with anyone but William. While he had done his habitual reconnaissance, she'd been swamped by guilt. She barely knew Emmett, yet her feelings for him were so strong, so vivid.

Now that she was touching him, she never wanted to let go. She introduced him to the others who shared the head table. It was a wonder watching him show such charm and relaxed polish when she knew the rough edges and constant vigilance lurking underneath.

As everyone took their seats, her daughter came up behind the head table. "Mom?"

"Is there a problem?"

"No. We were just hoping you'd come say hi." She tipped her head toward the table where Cecelia spotted Thomas glaring at Emmett.

"I'll be over once the formalities are done."

"Thanks," Casey looked relieved. "Uncle Thomas is twitchy."

"You can tell him I'm fine," Cecelia said, smiling as her daughter walked away.

Emmett leaned close to her. "What was that about?"

"That would be my overprotective detail." She patted his knee under the table, resisted the urge to leave her hand there. They weren't lovers, no matter how much she wanted him. They were hardly partners, though it had felt that way when he'd been sharing information this morning. "I had to tell her a bit more about you."

After the meeting in the café, Cecelia had been forced to give her daughter a detailed report of last night's altercations with Isely's men. It was the smart thing to do, if only so Casey could be better prepared for any more trouble.

She'd painted Emmett as the hero he'd been and Casey had been smart enough not to argue or imply her mother's perception was warped by circumstance.

"I've asked Casey to run interference for us tonight, so they won't hassle you. Much."

"Gee, thanks."

"She promised not to show them the picture."

"The picture?" He set his fork down carefully and blotted his mouth. "From last night?"

She nodded.

"Dancing at the marina?"

"That's the one."

She'd tried leaving out last night's more personal details until Casey had admitted getting a call from Heather. Even then, Cecelia tried to pin the girl's claims on a drunken stupor, but Casey had pulled out her phone and shown her the picture of the kiss.

Cecelia had nearly asked for a copy, but made the better choice and asked if her brother had seen it. Casey's denial had been sincere and full of concern, and nothing Cecelia said eased that worried look in her daughter's eyes.

Her throat went dry now just thinking about the picture, remembering how alive—how absolutely exhilarated—she'd felt in that moment when he'd kissed her in the middle of a party they hadn't been invited to.

"Nice effort, but it won't help." His eyes darted to the table in question. "They all know me."

"Know whatever you've led them to believe, anyway." She winked when he glared at her. "Let Casey handle them."

"If you say so."

"Lighten up. The salad isn't so bad." She took a bite and encouraged him to do the same. "It's the chicken you're likely to choke on."

"You're making chicken jokes. Why not just tell me about what happened while I was gone? Obviously something did."

"Nothing too dreadful."

"What exactly falls into that category?"

"We can discuss it later. I got the impression we'd have some time, just the two of us, this evening."

His silence was enough confirmation. Not that she needed it. When Isely's men grabbed her, she trusted him not to leave her with them for long. The idea had her shuddering inside. Having that monster touch her was enough to have her choking without a single bite of the chicken.

A waiter passed with a tray of champagne flutes, but Cecelia declined. Going tipsy on champagne wouldn't help her get through what she knew was coming.

She'd ignored the speculative looks Thomas aimed her way through the speeches and awards.

Had even tried provoking him a bit by holding Emmett's hand in full view once she'd delivered her gratitude to everyone who'd supported the cause. Yes, she was moving on, personally and professionally, and it was time for the world to adjust.

William was no doubt giving her a standing ovation from the place good men like him went.

For the first time since she'd said a final goodbye to her husband, she truly felt as if she was where she was meant to be.

No one, not that evil man Isely or anyone else, was going to take this from her.

When the orchestra started up, Thomas wasted no time in claiming her for the first dance. She nearly laughed at the complete lack of subtlety when Casey and Levi and Lucas and Victoria flanked them on the dance floor.

"I told you to stay away from him," Thomas said through a tight smile.

"In case you missed it, I'm a grown woman. I've had a husband and daughter and a whole life, Thomas."

"This is different. He's dangerous."

"I think I like that about him," she replied with shocking honesty. It was the rough edges under Emmett's polish that made him so appealing. She'd been raised to expect certain manners and behaviors from the men in her social sphere. While he could fit in anywhere the job demanded, she liked the man he was when they were alone best of all.

"That isn't funny, Lia. I've traced the leaks to his computer. He's a traitor."

"Of course he is." She laughed lightly just to keep up appearances. "I don't believe that. I know you have your pick of talented agents and would never snap up a dud."

"He sold secrets to a black-market weapons dealer."

She shook her head. "Take another look. He's only been a picture-perfect gentleman around me." She was ready for Thomas to call her on the lie, or the reference, but he was lost in his own gloomy thoughts.

"He wasn't an agent when I recruited him. Clearly I misjudged his abilities."

"Not from my perspective." She pinched his shoulder when he ignored her. "Listen to me. We were in real danger last night and he protected me. You should trust your first instincts where he is concerned."

"Where's your wedding band?"

She sighed. He wouldn't hear reason from her. Not on this. If he needed a gift for Jo or ideas for a brunch menu, she'd be his first call, but she'd never have his ear when it came to agents, business or covert operations.

"It's in the safe at the house," she replied.

"Where it has been since Casey's wedding." She was more pleased than she should have been by the shock on his face. "Where's your wife?"

"Working."

"Is that a politically correct way of saying she's in protective custody?"

"I should be so lucky."

Cecelia smiled. "So she refused, too?"

"She pointed out there wasn't an active threat on her."

Cecelia's mind leaped to the logical conclusion. "You have her looking for the mole." She hoped Jo would be objective enough to see what Emmett was really up to.

"Fresh eyes never hurt anything."

"True." Cecelia looked up into her big brother's face, studied every line he'd earned from the burdens and victories of his job. Why couldn't he see she wanted the same sense of accomplishment and purpose for her own life?

A not-so-small part of her wanted to tell him everything. To pull him aside and explain that she and Emmett had this whole threat under control. Or as much control as possible when the enemy was a madman bent on revenge.

"Thank you for being here," she said, kissing him lightly on the cheek. "I love you both. Tell Jo I said hello." She gave his hand a squeeze as the song ended. "That's my cue to mingle."

She stepped away before she did anything that could dilute the effect of tonight's looming drama. Whatever Isely had planned, she knew Emmett wouldn't let anything terrible happen to her or the people they both loved.

She grinned, thinking how adamantly he'd deny it if he'd heard her make such a statement. But she knew it was true. A man didn't do the things Emmett had done without love. For country, team or Thomas, there would be the logical, analytical reasons on the surface. But courage and conviction came from a noble place in the heart, and it took both to complete the lonely mission he'd taken on.

Chapter Thirteen

Emmett found her a few moments later and drew her out onto the floor for a waltz.

"A lie by omission is still a lie," she said.

His eyes were clouded as he met her gaze. "Whatever your brother said, you're stuck with me until this is over."

She was happy to hear it. "Not him. You. There was no mention of dancing on your profile, and yet you're quite talented."

"You're determined to be cheerful tonight." He flexed his fingers on her back and her body warmed to his touch. "You know I lie to everyone. That profile was geared to attract you."

"It worked." Too well, in fact. She was keeping it light, the epitome of a society matron reigning over a successful event, but she wanted some sign that what she was feeling for him wasn't one-sided. "Though a mention of dancing wouldn't have hurt."

She thought about the forest of untruths that

made up the landscape Emmett, her daughter and brother worked in. William had surely lied to her a thousand times by necessity through the course of their marriage. The mission-related untruths and alibis had never been an issue before, and she could only rationalize that it was now because she barely knew Emmett.

Except she felt like she knew him better than he knew himself.

They moved across the dance floor with the rest of the crowd, waltzing and smiling in a swirl of color and light.

Since discreet inquiries hadn't worked on him, she went for a direct approach. "So tell me what's true."

"This." He held her a bit too close through a turn and her breath caught with anticipation as her body met his from breast to thigh.

She gave him the smile the world would expect her to show and saw that he recognized the ploy.

"Now who's lying?"

"Part of the job, right?" She let the music carry her, embolden her. "What do you want most from me?"

He hesitated, but she gripped his shoulder and gave him a look warning him to shoot straight with her on this.

"More than you want to give, I'm sure."

The words, the husky voice gave her hope. She cocked an eyebrow. "Mission parameters first, please."

"First?"

She didn't dignify that with an explanation, simply waited for him to make his decision.

"Nothing has changed. Isely intends to kidnap you as leverage against your brother."

"And you're the kidnapper?"

"Would you prefer someone else? I can introduce you to the man in the corner who infiltrated hotel security for tonight."

When he turned her on the floor as gracefully as any contestant on that dancing reality show, she spotted the hulking brute he meant. He probably expected her to collapse in some fluttery, feminine panic. She didn't, though she wouldn't want to run up against that man in a dark alley, or anywhere else for that matter.

Emmett Holt was her only protection.

"How do you know?"

"I got him in."

She gasped and he drew her tight against him again as they swirled through another turn.

"You wanted the truth," he said.

She nodded. "If my kidnapping's on the schedule—" she met his gaze "—I'd rather go with you."

"Good choice."

She wasn't so sure. After kissing him last night for the sole purpose of surviving, she was all too aware that this man presented more than a few other dangers. Many of them far beyond physical.

Yes, she wanted to dance with him all night, to soak up the sensual delight she found in his embrace. It had been so long since anyone had held her like she mattered purely as a woman, since she'd been able to hold someone the same way.

William had traveled often for work, but those absences had given her just the briefest taste of loneliness. There'd been time for girlfriends, movie marathons or quiet nights with a good book and a bottle of wine.

She'd quickly learned none of those nights with friends, movies or books replaced the very real need for affectionate contact. For kisses, for...

"You're not listening."

She blinked several times, bringing his face into focus. "My apologies."

"First lesson for ops is to maintain your focus."

"Duly noted, thank you." She found it odd he was the only person of her acquaintance showing any acceptance of her career change. "I appreciate your support of my career plans," she said. "I know it's not your priority here."

The last strains of the music drifted away and they came to a stop with it, but he didn't quite release her. "Your life is my highest priority."

She felt something in her heart click as she looked into his eyes. The man just twisted her up inside. He'd lied, by all accounts was more than ready to use her without any remorse, but she couldn't seem to hold it against him. Knew she would never hold it against him.

People she'd known for far longer, her friends and family, said stay away, but she just couldn't. Especially not if a successful mission meant she had to spend time with that brute glowering at her from the corner.

"He just gave me the sign to move."

She hadn't seen a sign, but she was trying not to look that direction.

"Are you ready?" Emmett whispered.

She nodded, her throat too dry for words.

"Follow my lead."

Anywhere. She trusted him that much. He'd worked with her brother. He possessed more skills that she might ever learn.

He tucked her hand inside his elbow and steered her toward the head table. "Is there anyone else you need to speak with before we go?"

"Seriously?"

"Yes. I'm trying to make this as stress-free as possible for you."

"In that case, I should greet Lucas Camp and—"

"No." His muscles tensed—a physical emphasis of the quiet, stern refusal. "Anyone but him."

She gave a slight shake of her head. "Someone else will announce the silent auction winners when they can't find me."

"You have the gun with you as well as your phone?"

"GPS on as instructed."

"Good. We're done here."

She glanced up, saw his smile, but the warmth in it was suspect. Every move he made was calculated for their audience. She wondered if he realized they had that in common tonight.

She retrieved her purse and followed his lead as they aimed for an open bar station and the conversation area beyond.

They stepped out to the balcony area, where cocktails had been served. Trees planted in the lobby garden sparkled with holiday lights, branches reached toward the skylight above. The glass elevator serving the first five floors was wrapped with a bow like a present as it zipped up and down.

When they'd booked the Plaza for the gala, she'd seen the beauty and gracefulness of the design. She'd envisioned the perfect layout and the space full of guests eager to open their wallets for the chance to honor William's memory.

Tonight she saw shadows and threats where she should have only seen friends and donors.

"You need to brace yourself, Cecelia."

"You mean we can't just waltz all the way up to the suite and hide out with the convenience of room service?"

"Nope."

Those few minutes on the dance floor, wrapped in his embrace as the orchestra played, were so different from the heat and flash of last night's salsa. But the lingering result had been just as magical. Just as enticing.

"We can't show off more of our talent on the dance floor before disappearing?" she teased, mostly to quiet her nerves.

"It would make more of a scene," he agreed.

She grinned, just imagining the reaction. The poor, lonely Mrs. Manning never did anything as spontaneous as dance without the guide of music. What had happened to her, they would all wonder. They'd whisper behind their hands that she'd had some sort of breakdown. After last night's public display of heat—if not exactly affection with a virtual stranger—a similar uncharacteristic demonstration tonight might be enough to snap her perfectly respectable reputation in two.

She kind of liked the idea of being a wicked widow.

But that wasn't to be. She would simply vanish from the festivities, and those in attendance would speculate. She knew enough to understand how a report of her disappearance might go. Though for obvious reasons she didn't expect Thomas to report her missing. He had his own way of handling the situation. If there was trouble, any witnesses might call for security or the authorities. All the more reason they had to be discreet.

She could do this. For Thomas and Casey. For Emmett.

The men she assumed were Isely's crew had taken up stations on either end of their section of the balcony. She leaned closer to Emmett. No one but him would get a chance to do the kidnapping tonight.

She dug in her heels and drew them to a stop near the corner. Not at all out of sight of the crowd in the ballroom, but not as front and center as they'd been at last night's party. "Kiss me."

"Later. If you ask nicely," he said, his eyes locked on her lips.

She tugged his lapels. "Three o'clock and nine o'clock. You know they're there." This wasn't the time for nice. "Now kiss me."

Pressing her lips to his, she prayed he understood what she was after. She needed to leave no doubt that she was involved, willingly, with this man. Maybe he didn't care about his reputation, but she did.

He understood how to kiss; no room for doubt on that score. What she'd meant to be for show, to give the gossips something to chew on, turned into a banquet of sensations. Pinned between the wall and his equally unyielding body, she thrilled at the fascinating rush sizzling through her veins.

His wide palm cupped her cheek as he drew back a fraction of an inch. His breath was warm against her lips. She turned her face, pressing a kiss into his palm as she gauged the progress Isely's men had made.

"Once you're trained and in the field, no one will know you well enough to judge you," he murmured in her ear as he guided her past the elevator, around the balcony, toward the top of the wide staircase.

She wanted to ask how he'd guessed her earlier thoughts, but conversation, like kisses, would have to wait for later.

A door marked as a fire exit opened and the burly man from the ballroom waved them closer. Emmett deftly stepped around her, putting himself between her and Isely's man.

"This way," the man said, stepping into Emmett's path.

Emmett plowed a fist deep into the man's belly and pushed him back into the stairwell, yanking the door shut.

On the other side of the balcony, Cecelia's brother paused at the ballroom doors, his head swiveling from side to side. He was already searching for her.

She'd be hard to miss in this bold red gown. Next time she had kidnapping on the agenda, she'd wear something less flashy.

They reached the stairs and rushed down, and the fresh scent of the seasonal evergreens draped along the rails tickled her nose. The soft needles brushed her hand and caught at her wide skirt, but she kept moving forward. Oh, yes. Next time, a discreet gown and ballet flats. At this pace she'd be lucky if she didn't break an ankle and completely derail their plan.

"He hassled you, didn't he?" There had been a moment between dances when she'd lost sight of her brother. She suspected he'd had a word with Emmett. This wasn't exactly the time to carry on a casual conversation, but it kept her steady. "Thomas, I mean."

"If your brother had decided to act against me, I wouldn't be here."

She shivered at the thought. "Then what makes you so sure I'm worried about public opinion?" She was. Or always had been. But she was changing…slowly.

"You shouldn't be," he said. "The only opinion that ever matters is your own."

"A universal truth."

"That's me." He chuckled, checked behind them for trouble. "Moving to ops is a good call for you."

"You're probably still the only one who thinks

so," she said under her breath. Would these stairs never end?

Why was it those who loved her couldn't see how desperately she needed to change things up? Everyone thought they knew what she wanted, what she needed. Yet no one listened when she tried to explain her new goals and the catalyst behind them. Maybe that was part of the reason she needed to see this through rather than hide in protective custody.

Finally they reached the lobby. "What about my things?"

She'd packed a bag and left it in the suite, according to his instructions.

"Handled." He took her hand. "Stay close."

She should have known that would be all the warning he'd give.

A muffled pop sounded above them, followed by the startled shrieks of the crowd in the ballroom. Smoke poured from the center doorway.

"What did you do?"

"Diversion. No injuries."

"Lia!" Thomas shouted. Or maybe she just thought she heard her brother as Emmett ushered her out the front doors and into the cold night. Her heart sank just a little at the fear and worry she'd heard in those two syllables.

Stay alert, she ordered herself. No mistakes. No missteps. A front had moved in and rain with a chance of snow was expected over the weekend. She added a shrug or shawl to her mental list of things to wear at her next kidnapping. Her nerves calmed a bit with the mundane and totally ludicrous thoughts.

A gray sedan idled at the end of the Plaza's circular drive, as anonymous in this area as the black SUVs that escorted officials everywhere in DC.

Emmett opened the passenger door and helped her gather her dress inside. The only outward sign of his urgency was the way he raced around to the driver's side. She glanced to the hotel, spotted her brother and two men dressed in hotel uniforms. Specialists. It seemed several uninvited guests had joined the festivities. She wished she could call to Thomas and let him know she was okay.

"Where'd you get the car?" she asked, working hard to keep her voice steady.

"Courtesy of Isely." He pulled away from the Plaza. "Buckle up. We'll have a tail in no time."

"Which team?"

"Both, the way my night's been going. I'm sure each of them will believe they're an escort."

"What can I do?"

"Send your brother a text message. Tell him you're all right."

She pulled out her phone and sent more than one text message, hoping after that kiss one of her friends or family would assume what she wanted them to assume: that she was having a holiday affair.

Emmett cruised north through Old Town, toward the Beltway into Washington, D.C.

"We're not hiding in the marina, are we?"

"No." He slipped a phone out of his jacket and placed it on the console between them. "Let me know if any messages come through."

"Of course," she said, fishing her gun out of her purse.

"Ah, here we go."

A black car pulled up beside them and a voice ordered them to pull over. She sank back into the seat as Emmett floored it. He slipped in and out of traffic like he'd been raised by a pack of race-car drivers. That sense of danger she'd felt last night returned, bigger and more tempting than ever.

As did her brother's voice in her head telling her Holt was the problem child. She looked at her phone, wondering what message she could send to change his opinion.

"Ah, here comes the cavalry now."

She twisted in her seat and saw they were leading a parade of sorts. The black car was followed by a black SUV with blue-and-red flashing emergency lights.

"You want the police involved?" She thought police involvement was a bad thing.

"I don't much care as long as we lose the extra

personnel. If Mission Recovery intervenes tonight, I won't be able to stop Isely's endgame."

She came up hard against the door as he jerked the car around slower traffic. As she reached to steady herself, she bumped the handle and the door flew open.

"Cecelia!" He slowed down and reached over to grab her arm.

"I'm okay! Drive!" As he accelerated, the momentum helped her get the door closed, but there was no hope for the hem of her dress. "Damn it."

"Are you hurt?"

"No. I dropped the phone."

"No problem." He jerked them in front of the shelter of a semi-truck and then took the first available exit. It was the airport.

"Thought you wanted them to track it?"

"It's not the end of the world."

He suddenly slowed to the posted speed limit, causing her to lean forward against the seat. He circled the terminal.

"Please don't tell me I have to get this dress and a gun through security."

"It would be a good training exercise."

"Funny. I can't believe I dropped the phone."

"Really, it's okay. It was some amount of insurance, but not essential. Isely knows how to contact me. He'll tell me where he wants you to end up."

She was starting to get antsy about that. "I thought you made other arrangements."

"I did." He reached over and covered her hand with his. "We'll be fine. It appears he still trusts me."

"How can you be sure? He's tried a hostile take-over on your kidnapping assignment two nights running."

"I can't be certain. But I have what he wants. That's always the key, Cecelia. Always."

Her throat felt dry at the thought. She dismissed her fears. She trusted Emmett. "So what now?"

He pulled into a rental car lot and parked in the return lane. "Now we disappear for the evening. Should we go dancing?"

A smile spread across her lips. "Tempting as that is, I could really use a drink."

"Then drinks it is."

He took her hand as they left the car and hurried across the lot to the reservations side. With a swipe of a card, they were on their way again.

"Are you getting the hang of it?" he asked as they left the airport, heading into the heart of DC.

"You did part of this for my benefit."

"Two birds, one stone," he replied.

"I'm starting to realize just how much I have to learn."

"But you still *want* to learn?"

She paused, thinking over the past twenty-four

hours, comparing those hours to the entirety of her life up to this point. It might not have been a fair comparison, since the months of fighting an unwinnable battle against cancer was foremost in her mind. Still, she knew she had it in her to do more—to be more—than a face for various charities.

"More than ever," she admitted.

Chapter Fourteen

Holt had never heard sweeter words. "Then let's get some more practice."

"What do you have in mind?"

He checked the burner phone Isely had provided. "I want to know why he's not giving me an address."

"We still have that location just off the coast."

"I know. I researched the wharfs and docks near Alexandria and on the Atlantic and came up with nothing I could tie to Isely."

"What about known associates with shipping or import interests here?"

He liked that they'd been thinking along the same lines. "Nada. He doesn't have any."

"Everyone has someone."

Not me. True or not, even in the privacy of his head the thought sounded pathetic.

"The only people I can put with him are his own crew. This job is personal. You as a target proves that."

"Maybe he forgot to send you the memo that he wants to kidnap me personally. Maybe it really has nothing to do with Thomas or Mission Recovery."

He shook his head. "Unless your husband left something crucial in your care that neither I nor Mission Recovery has learned of, that's not possible."

"But you can't know for sure," she argued.

"That's the one thing I am sure about," he guaranteed.

He drove in silence the rest of the way. Arguing with her would be a distraction he didn't need. This was about Isely and his need for vengeance against Thomas Casey and Mission Recovery. End of story.

When he reached the destination, he braced for the next part in his plan. He'd never had such trouble staying in the right frame of mind on a mission.

He started to get out of the car, but she stopped him with a soft touch on his sleeve. "What's the story here?"

"No story. Just another party. Smile," he said as the valet opened her door.

Outside the car he handed over the keys and wrapped his arm around her trim waist.

She followed his instruction to the letter. Somehow that made his heart glad, and there simply was no explanation why. She was a marvel, he decided. An uncommon blend of tenacity and bravery with a hearty lust for adventure. And her body... Well, he'd be better off if he put that out of his mind.

He paused in the lobby for a quick kiss. "This is an office party of sorts. You'll recognize a few faces from Casey's wedding."

"You're taking me into a room full of Specialists?"

"Well, a few folks are from the CIA, too."

She paled. "Why take the risk?"

"Because I need to get some rather sensitive information and showing up here as a couple supports the torrid affair gossip you started last night."

Her eyes narrowed, the blue spheres full of fire. It was an immediate turn-on. "That wasn't all my fault."

"I was perfectly respectable before we met," he lied with a wink. "We won't stay long. Can't stay long," he corrected. "No matter who asks, do not leave my side."

"Yes, sir."

He studied her face, gave her a glimpse of the raw need she stirred in him. "I could get used to that."

"Don't count on it."

Damn, he admired her spunk. He wanted to laugh, wanted to see just how far he could tease her before one of them gave in. But that wasn't on the agenda, no matter how hot and inspired he felt when she kissed him. The woman deserved a far better man than he was. She deserved her shot at ops, too, and he meant to see that she got it.

"Ready?"

She nodded, but her smile wobbled. Not acceptable. He stroked his hand across the bare skin of her shoulders and praised her dress designer. When she looked up at him again, he dropped a featherlight kiss on those perfect, rosy lips. "For courage," he said, then he turned toward the private reception taking up the entirety of the Irish-themed hotel bar.

More than half of the gathering was connected to Mission Recovery, and the hush that fell across the room when they saw him was palpable.

No, he didn't do social events and they all knew it. To arrive at all was unprecedented. To arrive with a date might be a portent of doom. For him in particular, if Director Casey had shared his suspicions with any one of the Specialists in attendance.

Since this was a party to celebrate the recent marriage of Specialist Jason Grant and his CIA wife, Gin Olin, he wasn't surprised when several people also recognized Cecelia.

"Stay with me," he reminded her behind a tense smile. If the way she was gripping his arm was any indicator, she had no intention of leaving his side.

The crowd parted for Jason and Gin as they

welcomed Holt and Cecelia, drawing them inside toward the bar.

Gin called for champagne, shot Holt a curious look over Cecelia's head then the women were immediately engrossed in conversation.

Holt made a mental note to ask Cecelia how she knew Gin. He'd long ago given up trying to understand women, but even he recognized that kind of bonding was too quick under the circumstances.

He accepted the champagne Grant offered, though he was ready for something with more bite and less fizz. Ah, well, that's why he had a bottle of Scotch on his boat waiting for a victory toast the moment he buried Isely.

"You said you had something?"

"The man credited with the virus is dead." Grant said this as if he'd given the newest weather report.

"How?"

"Self-inflicted gunshot wound. Five years ago."

Holt sipped, ignoring the annoying bubbles in the wine. "Guilt after the sale?"

"Or designed to look that way."

"What about his lab, notes, apprentices?"

"As far as I've been able to dig, all of his work is just gone."

"A targeted strike?"

Jason nodded. "That's my guess. But it wasn't our team, as you well know."

Then why wasn't Isely trying to get more money for a limited-edition bioweapon? The vial Isely had given to Holt was worth millions, assuming the virus was still potent.

"I came across something I believe you and your lovely wife will appreciate," Holt said. "Forgive the lack of wrapping." He withdrew a long, slim box from his inner pocket and handed it to Jason. "Congratulations. You and your wife should open it later. It's one of a kind."

Jason pocketed the box and raised his glass in salute. "We'll enjoy it, I'm sure."

Using the mirror, Holt eyed the crowded bar in an attempt to pinpoint which Specialists weren't here and which ones were watching him too closely. He gave up after a moment. It wasn't worth the effort. Any one of them, if not all of those present, had likely notified the director of his arrival already. The moment he and Cecelia walked out of here, he'd be a target again.

"Everything okay, sir?"

"A word of advice, Grant?"

"Please."

"Always make time for two things: your wife and a hobby." It was the only tip he could offer and the only attempt he'd make to clear his name.

If Grant understood, Holt might have a job to return to once Isely was contained. If the man didn't understand the message...well that's why he had the boat.

Holt turned to Cecelia, couldn't resist running his fingers down the back of her arm. "Time to go," he said.

She gave Gin a quick hug and then put her hand in his. "Lead on."

He wanted to go out the back but figured their odds were better in the lobby. The more people who saw them take the elevator upstairs, the better.

She was quiet as they waited.

"How do you know Grant's wife?" he asked as the car arrived and they stepped inside. He pressed the button for the seventh floor.

"It's a vague acquaintance."

Her eyes were clouded and he knew she was a bit lost in her past. A kiss wouldn't snap her out of it, though he was willing to try, but he thought she needed something. He rubbed her hand between his. For her, he told himself. Not because he felt the strange urge to comfort and soothe.

He didn't do the tender emotions. Until he'd met her, he didn't think he'd ever want to try. He tried to look at her objectively, but just couldn't anymore.

The doors parted on the seventh floor and he stepped out, only to get blindsided by a fist to the face. He reeled back into Cecelia's soft body, knocking her into the safety of the elevator.

He lunged at his attacker, taking the fight away from her. They hadn't discussed it, but with her brother's team downstairs, surely she'd go to them for help.

The man tried to sweep his foot in a takedown, but Holt twisted and blocked, gaining a brief advantage with an elbow strike that separated them. It was a relief to see his opponent was one of Isely's men, but the relief faded swiftly when he recognized which one.

The crew called him Thor for his long blond hair, broad build and hands as big as hammers. "Hand her over."

Holt spread his hands wide. "Who?"

Thor looked over Holt's shoulder, then ripped off what must have been an inspired combination of curses in German. But it wasn't enough to distract Holt from the fists racing toward his face.

He bobbed and weaved, ducking under one swing to bounce a jab off of Thor's sternum. Not much effect. He jerked back so Thor's next punch glanced off his jaw, but even that was enough to knock him off balance.

He staggered, then gave in and somersaulted backwards, bouncing back up to his feet. Thor closed in again. "She's mine to deliver," Holt said, hoping to goad Thor into sharing pertinent details. "I need the bonus."

He jabbed, ready to follow with a hook and left himself open to a devastating punch to the ribcage. Thor's cocky smile was worth the pain. Sort of.

The elevator chimed and both men turned. Cecelia stepped out into the hallway. "Leave him alone," she said, raising the revolver.

"Feisty," Thor said with an approving grimace. Grabbing Holt by the shirt, he turned, using him as a shield. "I see why you don't want to let her go."

Holt didn't bother explaining that Isely hadn't yet told him where to take her. "Downstairs," he snarled over his shoulder at Cecelia.

"Not without you," she replied, pulling the trigger.

The shot went wide, plowing into a framed print on the wall, but it was enough to startle Thor, who ducked away from the exploding glass.

Holt thrust his arms up and out, breaking Thor's hold. Rushing to Cecelia, he caught her at the waist and propelled her down the hall.

Another gunshot sounded, and chunks of wall exploded near his hip as they tumbled through the door into the stairwell.

"Down," he barked.

"Which floor?"

"Just keep going," he answered. There was a

bridge to the parking garage on four. Her heels clattered against the cement stairs and he couldn't tell if there was anyone following or not. With every landing they passed without the assault of more bullets, a flicker of hope spurred him on.

"Here," he said when they reached the fourth-floor landing. He paused only long enough to see the way was clear, then he took her hand. "Breathe. The car is close by."

Her eyes were wide and a little wild, but she nodded, her skirt rustling as she rushed to keep up with him.

Holt prayed he wasn't leading her into another trap, but the car he'd parked here last week was registered with a member of the hotel staff. He'd bribed a bartender, who needed both a car and extra cash to cover a gambling debt.

As much as he'd coached her to stay calm, Holt didn't take an easy breath until they were back on the parkway and headed to the grungy little motel he'd booked under yet another alias.

"I'm sorry."

He glanced over when he heard the quiver in her voice. "For what? You saved us."

"I should have hit him."

"Rookie mistake. It happens."

"Oh, Emmett. You really didn't look up every-thing, did you?"

He'd looked up plenty, nearly picked apart her

life. But then as a CIA family, she would know how to hide plenty. "What do you mean?"

"My husband and I used to go shooting for fun. Casey was three when she made her first trip with us. I'm no sharpshooter, but I'm pretty darned good."

He wasn't sure he wanted to hear about her husband, though he realized he'd made a critical error by not digging deeper into their married life. He wanted to classify it as irrelevant, but he knew now it had just been too uncomfortable.

"So why didn't you take Thor out?"

"He was moving erratically. I was worried about hitting you. I mean, I'm a pretty good shot, but not that good."

"Real life isn't the same as a paper target."

"Thanks, I hadn't noticed."

He reached for her, but she drew her hand away. "I'm not trying to patronize you, Cecelia. You have what it takes, but for the record, I can take care of myself."

"That's obvious." She shifted, staring out the window.

"You could have gone downstairs for help."

"I thought about it. But Isely sends men in pairs."

"You noticed. Good job."

"Hard to miss," she muttered. "I was terrified to think what might happen if they caught me first."

"You have everything the CIA wants in an agent."

"Right."

"You do." He reached over and covered her hand. "First of all, I wouldn't have let him take you. Second, that was my mistake back there for not clearing the hallway at the elevator. Learn from my mistake."

"Okay."

He didn't think she was convinced. "As for what you'd do if captured by Isely, I'm sure he'd be unhappy with your determination and resourcefulness."

"Maybe."

"Believe me. I've been at this longer than you."

She was quiet for a long time, and he hoped she was processing his praise while she replayed the last hour.

"Where are we going?"

"I have a reservation they shouldn't be able to track down," he replied. "We need some time to rest and regroup."

"Neither side will be pleased with our disappearance."

"Nope. But only one will get nasty about it."

"Isely."

"Yup."

Chapter Fifteen

As he pulled into the parking lot, he regretted choosing a cut-rate place like this one. She'd been through an ordeal and she deserved finer things than he would offer her tonight.

"Are we here?"

He nodded, wishing they were anywhere else. "Cash works here."

"And cash is untraceable." She reached out and caught his hand. "It's smart. Contrary to popular opinion, I don't need five-star accommodations all the time. Thank you for protecting me."

When she looked at him that way, protection wasn't what he wanted to give her. He leashed his unruly desire and led her through the back door and up to their room for tonight.

The door closed and her warm scent filled the small space. "Your things are by the dresser."

"Thanks. I'd like to change."

"In a minute." He had to focus on business. The mission. Anything but the thought of being near her when she removed that dress. "Now that we're alone, you need to tell me what happened today." He knew there was something, and she'd asked that question about this being about her instead of her brother.

"Do we have to do that now?" She reached up and removed the elegant jeweled choker. "You said rest and regroup. Surely it can wait a few hours."

He inhaled and shoved his hands into his pockets before he grabbed her and tossed that voluminous skirt up over her head. She needed his respect on a professional level, and somehow he couldn't not give it. "Does whatever happened pose an immediate threat?"

"Not unless they can find us."

"They being?"

"Isely."

"He has no idea where we are and I've sent him a message that I want to meet tomorrow."

"To turn me over."

"Of course, but—"

"I trust you to have a plan. Tell me later. Let's rest. And regroup."

Any argument he might have offered fled as she raised her hands to her hair, her full breasts testing the limits of her strapless gown. It was an entirely underrated form of torture to watch her free those long blond locks from the sleek, upswept style she'd worn all night. And she had a point. They were both mentally and physically exhausted.

He might have fantasized about the elegant stretch of her neck a little longer, but suddenly his fingers itched to fist in her hair.

Beware was right, he thought, staring at her. Isely had given the warning for an entirely different purpose, but it couldn't be more appropriate than right here in this room.

She gave him her back, drawing her hair forward over her shoulder. "A little help?" she asked, glancing over one bare shoulder.

Her lashes lowered, but her blue eyes smoldered. She was clearly daring him to help her out of the gown. He wasn't strong enough to resist.

He found the small hook at the top and released it, but the line of tiny buttons down her back posed a new temptation. He swallowed.

She was a siren and he'd willingly dash himself against the rocks for this moment with her. His fingers trembled as he loosened each button, revealing her skin one slow, beautiful inch at a time.

She was the most delectable present he'd ever had the pleasure of unwrapping.

His cynical arguments about holiday attire turned into an instant appreciation as the festive red of her lingerie against her creamy skin stoked the fire already raging inside him.

His fingers brushed along her spine, resting at the curve of her bottom as the last button popped free.

Desire slid through his system in a warm rush as she let the dress fall to the floor. She turned to face him and his knees threatened to buckle. She was a vision beyond his ability to imagine, her breasts barely contained in those hot red cups of shimmering fabric, the matching panties a wonderful target dividing the creamy skin of her midriff and thighs. But the lace-topped stockings in lethal black nearly stopped his heart.

Who would've guessed the prim, perfectly coiffed Widow Manning had an arsenal like this?

Of all the pictures he'd used to export hidden data, this would have been his favorite.

But definitely the least effective. He nearly laughed thinking of how the director would delete this one immediately—or kill him for having it at all.

Didn't matter. This image of her was burned into Holt's mind and would be there the rest of his days—no matter how few or how many remained.

"You're frowning," she said, taking a step closer.

He smiled, but it took work. "You're so damned beautiful." He drew back a step, cursed himself for being a coward. "We shouldn't do this."

"I disagree."

Of course she would. But it was a mistake, more

on her part than his. He just needed to redirect enough blood flow to his brain to think of it. Raw need for her was riding him too hard. His control was nearly shredded. He knew he couldn't hold out. Better she had informed consent here.

"I don't want to be gentle with you." He wanted to scare her a bit, wanted to back her off so he could regain his balance. But it wasn't fear or worry he saw in her eyes, it was...anticipation.

God help him.

"So don't be gentle." She took another step and her red bra brushed against the white of his tuxedo shirt, making his pulse jump. She tugged the ends of his bow tie and slid it out of his collar.

"Cecelia." It was the only coherent word he could get past his lips.

"I'm right here."

He knew that. Her fragrance crashed over him in vivid, sensual waves. The things he wanted to do to that body...the things he wanted her to do to him.

Her hands gripped his shirt and she tugged, popping the studs free. Her white-tipped fingernails scraped lightly across his chest. Her gasp proved plenty of reward for all those hard workouts.

"I'm not that white knight you're looking for," he said with an ache that almost undid him.

"I don't care." She flatted her hands on his skin and smoothed those silky palms over his chest.

He groaned. She was killing him, but a woman like Cecelia deserved tenderness from a gentleman with an Ivy League degree and the manners to match. Not the hot, rough, fast kind of sex he craved tonight. His hands hovered at her waist to set her away. His mind told him to behave but his body argued just the opposite.

She took his hands in hers and pressed the palms down against her soft flesh. He stopped breathing as she dragged them up her sides to cup her full breasts. Her nipples peaked under his palms and she used his hands to squeeze and caress them as she arched into his touch.

Keeping one of his hands trapped between hers and one full breast, she raised the other to her face and drew his thumb into her mouth, sucking hard then giving the sensitive pad a light nip.

He wasn't sure his heart could take much more.

"I'm not fragile, Emmett."

He hoped she meant it. He bent his head to kiss her. Hard. Her lips parted and her tongue tangled with his. She tasted of champagne and a shocking dark desire that matched his.

Reaching lower, he palmed her bottom and then hitched her up, beyond pleased when she wrapped her legs around his waist. She rocked her hips, grinding herself against him. As if he wasn't aroused enough, she gave a sigh of sheer pleasure.

No turning back now.

He'd be lucky if he could find his way to the bed. The world with all its complications and consequences just didn't exist beyond the woman in his arms. He dropped her to the bed and her laughter spurred him on as he stripped away his shirt and slacks. The view of her in that sexy lingerie made him as hard as he'd ever been.

"No," he rasped as she started to push off one of her strappy high-heel shoes. "Leave them on."

Her blue eyes sparkled and the curve of her lips was nothing short of wicked. "As you wish."

He watched her eyes travel over his body, enjoying her obvious appreciation of the view he presented. One she liked, apparently. The idea spurred his confidence—something he'd never needed before.

He knelt between her parted legs, then traced the lacy tops of her stockings. First with his fingers, then his mouth. He planted hot kisses across her bare belly, taking his time as he freed her lush breasts from that bra. She speared her hands into his hair, holding him close. He made a study out of the curve of her throat until finally claiming her mouth. She opened under him, her tongue stroking his as her hands explored his body.

He was so close to the edge already. He tore her

panties aside and found her wet and ready. When he pressed his fingers deep inside her, she bucked against his hand and her body arched. Moments later she cried out with a hard climax.

His eyes locked with hers as he gripped her hips. She rose to meet him and he drove himself into her with one swift thrust. Her body clutched around him as he gave in to the heavy rhythm pushing him. Those sexy heels dug into his hips as she tightened her legs around him. Her hands fisted in the linen; her eyes were dark with passion.

She moaned his name and he felt like a god at the sound. Her body strung tight as she reached her next climax. This one dragged him over the edge with her, and he thrust deep one last time before he sagged against the mattress.

HE WAS WAY better than some fantasy about a white knight, Cecelia thought as she drew the sheet up over her body. The cool air chilled her skin as her heart rate returned to normal. She wanted to burrow closer to Emmett's warmth, but he wasn't giving off an inviting vibe. She settled for resting her fingers lightly on his arm.

It wasn't as though she expected a declaration of love. She didn't think she was capable of giving him one. They were two consenting adults who'd given in to a mutually intense attraction and need. Simple. Straightforward.

Stockholm syndrome.

The idea made her giggle. She wasn't his prisoner any more than he was hers. Maybe the intensity of the whole situation had rendered her helpless. She just wanted to laugh at it all. She'd just made love with a man besides the one she'd been married to for twenty-five years. She had lost the shadow of widowhood just now…somehow. Kind of like losing her virginity with William. The whole idea had her shaking with the need to laugh. Tears welled in the corners of her eyes. Dear God, she was hysterical.

"That's not what a man wants to hear about now," he murmured, rolling to his side, stretching his arm under her pillow. His eyes sparkled in the light of the lamp by the table, but a darkness still shadowed his face.

"It's not you, it's me. Is that better?"

"Not really." He smoothed her hair away from her face. "What were you thinking that made you laugh?"

She sighed into his touch even as she sent her fingers roaming across that magnificent chest. "I was thinking about rapid-onset Stockholm syndrome."

"You know you're free to go anytime," he reminded her unnecessarily.

She smoothed her fingertips across his brow, easing the frown. Going might be a viable option, but it wouldn't be the prudent choice. Not just because she wasn't done with him, but because she didn't think she could outwit the enemy on her own. And she wasn't leaving him to do that on his own, either.

Tonight's adventure proved once more he was caught in a vise, and she refused to leave him to deal with it alone. Despite being chased by both her brother's team and Isely's men, the biggest obstacle she could see was Emmett himself. When would he open up and give her enough information to help?

He shocked her, bringing his face close and rubbing her nose with his. It was an unexpected tenderness from a man who claimed with body and words he wasn't capable of such things.

"You're still thinking." His thumb caressed the furrow between her brows.

No amount of wrinkle cream would ever completely erase the tiny lines there. She was well into forty...middle-aged. Was this part of her crisis?

"I am."

"That may be worse than the giggles."

He rolled to his back again and she immediately missed the heat of his body, the hard planes and thick ropes of his muscles against her more pliant frame. No matter what happened in the coming hours, she wouldn't have traded this stunning, sexy moment for any amount of caution or safety.

"Don't worry. I was just thinking that *this* was worth all the rumors we've no doubt started. But I'm not in the mood for pillow talk." Not yet. She shifted closer to him, pressed her lips to the crisp hair of his chest.

"You're not?"

"Nope," she whispered against his skin, and was rewarded when he trembled as she worked her way down to his navel, and lower still. "Not even close."

Chapter Sixteen

Holt slipped out of Cecelia's warm embrace and peered around in the darkness until he found his discarded tuxedo pants on the floor. Pulling them on, he went and turned on his laptop, hoping to find some good news to share with her when she woke up.

Sometime after their third round, they'd managed to turn off the lights and sleep. He hadn't felt this rested in months. It should have been a comfort, but it worried him. Cecelia wasn't meant to be part of his future. And right now he couldn't imagine her not in it.

He turned his back to her so he could focus on the mission instead of the glorious temptation of her body. He logged into the email account he used only for Isely. Judging by the messages, the bastard had had a grand time watching Thomas angst over Cecelia's disappearance. A terse acceptance was his only acknowledgement of the meeting Emmett had requested.

He scanned local news headlines online rather than risk waking her with the television. No one had reported her disappearance as a kidnapping, but it was hardly a victory. After months of behaving with a single-minded, ruthless efficiency, now Isely was unpredictable, changing the rules of the game at the last minute.

The bastard had been thinking it over for months and had finally come to the conclusion that something was wrong with the virus. Now that Holt knew the biologist was dead, it only added to the mystery. A bioweapon was a powerful thing, and Isely was just too damned casual about it. The man had thrown a fit and promised retribution when the CIA had grabbed one of the two remaining vials in Vegas last month, but Holt didn't believe the performance.

"Working already?"

He hadn't heard her leave the bed, more proof he was far too comfortable with her.

"Yeah."

"I'll make coffee." Her hands rested lightly on his shoulders and her hair teased the bare skin of his shoulders when she leaned forward to kiss his cheek. "Did he agree to the meeting?"

"Yes." He realized he didn't want to lie to her. "But he's not happy about it."

"No surprise."

"Yeah." He watched her walk toward the little niche where the coffeemaker, microwave and minifridge were clustered together. She was wearing his tuxedo shirt and nothing else. He was instantly hard for her, all too ready to forget enemy plans, betrayals and furious brothers who knew a dozen ways to kill a man without leaving trace evidence.

"Would you please tell me more about Isely? So I'm ready for the meet," she coaxed.

"Why? Having sex doesn't make us a team." He said this as coldly as possible.

She turned, crossed her arms and made that shirt ride up a bit higher on her thighs. "I asked you to stop doing that."

He stood up, stretching his arms over his head, his eyes never leaving hers. "I shouldn't have to push you away. You should have the good sense to run."

She licked her lips. "I know who's who in this little drama."

"You do?"

She nodded. "I ran from the bad guys last night." She blatantly looked him over from head to toe and back again. "And right into your arms." She walked over and wound her arms around him. It wasn't anything like yesterday's hug, as they were both wearing considerably less this time. "You're beautiful."

"Flattery? That's your next tactic? Sweetheart, it's no use. I know I'm gorgeous."

"Keep it up," she said, giving the back of his arm a hard pinch.

"Ow!" But he couldn't help laughing, then he stopped short, trying to recall the last time he'd really laughed. He couldn't bring a recent memory to mind, not to mention a moment of shared laughter with a woman. "Why does it matter? As long as you're safe and I get the job done, you don't need to worry about Isely."

"Thomas said something last night."

"About Isely?" *Please let it be about Isely.*

"More about teamwork. He said fresh eyes never hurt."

Couldn't argue that adage. "He's right. Maybe you can find a reason for Isely's abrupt change of behavior."

She poured them both a cup of coffee and joined him at the small table. "So talk."

"This is all still classified—"

"My clearance is current and this place isn't bugged." She shuddered. "Unless they're bed bugs."

"Ease up," he said, patting her knee. "I'm going

down regardless. I just want you to know what not to say when you're rescued."

She rolled her eyes at him. "Just talk. Tell me about Isely. And maybe I'll tell you some things."

"Five years ago, Thomas infiltrated the Isely group and interrupted the first scheduled sale of a lethal new virus. Isely's father got killed in the crossfire when the deal was blown. The vials Thomas turned in when he got back to the States weren't any deadlier than a saline solution."

She frowned. "But Thomas would never have kept a deadly bioweapon."

"When the deal went sideways, everyone assumed Isely had planned to double-cross his original buyer all along. The reports Thomas filed on the operation were verified, and nothing more came of it until a few months ago when a deadly strain of flu wiped out a remote village in the Middle East."

"That was on the Pakistan border, right?"

"Good guess."

She shrugged. "I heard about it through other channels."

"Other channels," he echoed.

She leaned forward and her shirt gaped, giving him a distracting view of her cleavage. "You know exactly where I've spent my low-profile career. And knowing that along with who my husband was, you find it surprising I've made a few connections through the years? Please."

"I didn't give that much thought." When this had started, he hadn't thought about her husband because he wasn't relevant to the situation. After spending time with her online and especially after last night, Holt didn't want to think about her husband at all.

It was a double standard considering his storied and colorful past, but a relationship wasn't in their future. No way would she stick by him if he survived long enough to be charged with working for Isely. She was accustomed to heroes and good guys, not that gray place he represented.

His possessiveness for her was irrational and unexpected. It wasn't even based in reality. He'd started an online relationship as a means to an end. But he didn't want it to end.

"Hey."

He glanced down to where her palm gently covered his knee. His whole body reacted, zeroing in on that small point of contact. His pulse kicked, his breath hitched and his hands warmed with the urge to touch and take. He shook his head and gulped air deep into his lungs.

"Sorry. Wandering thoughts," he muttered.

"You've been working undercover for too long. Who else knows about your mission?"

"No one. That's just it. No one else in Mission

Recovery was cleared on the Germany job. Despite that, no one could know or Isely would never have taken the bait."

She sat back, taking her warmth with her, and he knew she was doubting his story. And why shouldn't she? It was his word against the evidence. Evidence he'd purposely stacked against himself to keep Isely on the hook.

"Then why did we meet with Jason and Gin?"

"He doesn't know how far I've gone," Holt insisted. "I only asked him to look up the biologist who created the virus. And I handed over the last vial of the virus Isely gave me weeks ago."

She stared at him but he couldn't read her at all. "You'd better tell me everything. And fast," she warned.

Somehow he found himself answering to her demand. Way, way outside his normal protocol. "I wasn't supposed to see him again ever. It was kidnap you, deliver you to the address he chose and I'd be out."

"But you went on the offensive and demanded a meeting instead."

"Correct."

"And you don't have any idea what he was going to do with me?"

"The way I put it together, kidnapping you puts me in the rogue-agent category, which embarrasses the director and jeopardizes his career. Isely can also use your capture to further expose and antagonize your brother."

"Right." She sipped her coffee. "What about the virus?"

"I dispersed that last night at the gala."

"You did what?"

The flash of horror on her face proved he'd finally found the one thing to push her away. He regretted it instantly. "Isely wanted the virus dispersed at the gala so it would cause more blowback for Thomas. I arranged it so a couple of his guys were on the security detail, remember?"

"Yes." Her horrified reaction had already reverted back to what he considered her crisis face. The still, serene expression effectively concealed how fast her mind was working through the problem at hand. He wondered when she'd act on the disgust and fury she must be feeling.

"One of his men was supposed to contaminate someone or something. If the virus works as advertised, later tonight people will show symptoms and eventually a good many of them will die."

"And pathology will show it was a designer strain of the flu and call it a terrorist attack."

"Yes. The people who matter in the intelligence community will link it back to your brother and blame him because it happened on his watch."

"Isely gave this a great deal of thought."

"He's been working it out for years. Colorado, Vegas, those were just building blocks for last night."

"But…"

"Why do you assume there's a 'but'?"

She simply stared at him, waited him out. He supposed it was a dumb question. For whatever reason, she didn't view him the way the rest of the world viewed him—as a spook too quiet and withdrawn for his own good.

"I met the courier, let him inject me with the virus and then returned to the party. I danced and mingled and they reported it to Isely. Later I sent the remaining product and a blood sample to the lab."

"How?"

"My assistant was close by."

"But you never left the gala."

He smiled. "Only for a moment. I'm quick and I have good hands."

"Yes, you do." She traced the rim of her coffee cup with her fingertip. "What did you inject instead of the virus?"

"I used one of the bogus vials Thomas originally brought back." He waved his hands in the air. "Hand is quicker than the eye."

"Apparently." She uncurled from the chair and

poured more coffee into her cup. "Sounds like you've got this under control."

"Everything but Isely's sudden urgency."

"He tried to jump the gun on the kidnapping but didn't succeed, so you're back on schedule, right?"

He shook his head. "It will fall apart when no one gets sick. And that possible exchange at sea is all wrong." He paced away from her.

"Talk to me, Emmett. Let me help. You're not giving me everything."

What the hell was he doing? But he couldn't not tell her everything. "He knows the virus is useless. He has to. He just doesn't care about it enough."

"But it wiped out those villagers."

"I can't explain that. Maybe it breaks down. Maybe they used a different formula."

"Is there anyone here in the States who can help him with the virus?"

"Probably, but he hasn't made contact. My gut is telling me we're in serious trouble here. If I leave you alone to go to the meet, either Mission Recovery or Isely's crew will find you. Isely will learn this quickly, and then we'll never know what he's up to."

"So take me along."

"What, like a date?"

"No, like a partner who has your back."

"You're not trained for that."

"My fresh eyes see it as your only option. You

go alone, you walk into a trap and I'm stuck dealing with him."

He shook his head.

"Emmett, are you this good at everything you do?"

"What do you mean?"

"You purposely painted yourself into a corner. Who were you going to hand over to Isely in my place? What was your exit strategy?"

He scrubbed at his face and braced for her shock and righteous indignation. "Originally, I'd planned to hand you over, but with a GPS tag so I could follow you. Everything the director needed to clear himself and protect the team is scheduled to automatically dump into his inbox after the exchange. A precaution in case I lost your trail. You probably don't believe me, but I wouldn't have let them hurt you."

"I believe you."

He wanted to believe her, but anything might be going on behind her crisis face. "But now, with Isely shifting the plan…"

"You don't trust your own instincts or your own decisions."

"Something like that."

"Well, the man has reason to hate Thomas, and it's obvious he wants him to suffer. How did you get yourself between them?"

"Just doing my job."

"Emmett, if you don't start sharing what's really on your mind, I can't help you sort out the solution."

"The best solution is for you to go into protective custody with Mission Recovery while I take down Isely at the meet. The evidence will show up on schedule. Combined with what I've told you, Thomas will be satisfied and safe."

"That sounds like the easiest and prettiest solution, but it might not be the best."

CECELIA STRUGGLED NOT to flinch under the weight of that iron stare. She wasn't about to let him take the fall for this, not when he'd so selflessly given himself to protect her and her brother.

Her feelings were a tangled mess of guilt, expectations, lust and fragile new hope, but one thing was clear. Emmett needed her. Even more astounding, she knew she could be helpful, even if he didn't give her more insight.

Isely thought she knew something. She just had to figure out how to use that to help Emmett. If she dared tell him about that meet, he would definitely lock her away just as Thomas had wanted to. How could she help anyone then?

While the work she did for the CIA was straightforward and boring, she'd been honest with Emmett about making connections.

She should probably consult her daughter, but

that would only negate the text message she'd sent last night declaring she was fine and wishing her and Levi a Merry Christmas.

"How old is Isely?" she asked, trying hard to reconcile anything Emmett knew with something she might know and not realize the importance of.

"Thirty-four in January."

She did the math. "So his father's death hit him at a prime point in his career development. Is he married?"

"No."

Too bad. The man had nothing to lose, no serious distraction from planning this detailed revenge. It made him more dangerous. "Other family?"

"His mother and a few cousins."

"Religious at all?"

"Catholic," Emmett snapped, glaring at her. "Stop grasping at straws. The man's been profiled already."

"You said he's breaking behavior patterns. I'm trying to find the angle."

"You're trying to find the place where he recruited me."

The way he saw through her was a bit unnerving, but she took comfort that he wasn't discounting her ability to analyze and assess a complex situation. "Wouldn't have to go fishing if you'd just tell me."

She smiled, but his eyes went flat and cold and his jaw tensed. The man could put up brick walls faster than anyone she'd ever met. Well, maybe except for Thomas. How could she convince him he wasn't alone in this anymore?

She wanted to believe they'd started something last night, long before that, really. Foolish as it might be, she wanted more than a wild, brief affair.

After William, she hadn't thought she'd bother with anything lasting again. Hot and thrilling had been the plan. But maybe she wasn't wired that way after all. Or maybe she was one of the lucky women who bumped into two good men in one lifetime.

It was abundantly clear Emmett didn't see himself as good guy or keeper material. There were skeletons in his closet, she was sure, but everyone had a past. She didn't have any desire to go digging them up, but she'd be more than willing to help him clear them out if and when he felt so inclined.

When his profile had popped on the online dating site, she'd had the option to dig and had refrained. Sometimes too much information was just that—too much information.

She'd wanted a bit of mystery in the men who'd expressed interest in her profile. Wanted the fun of discovery that came with meeting someone new.

Well, she'd gotten plenty of both with Emmett Holt. And now they were at a standoff.

"About yesterday." If she expected him to provide full disclosure, she had to do the same no matter if he attempted to get her into protective custody. She'd stood her ground with Thomas and she would stand it with him.

Emmett pierced her with a sharp gaze.

"Isely came to see me at the hotel."

"You didn't call." He stalked closer, leaned forward and caged her in the chair.

"I had the phone on and I was ready to press the number." Her voice cracked. "Casey was watching the whole time." She chose not to mention Isely's threat against her daughter. Or the stupid choice he'd asked her to make.

"What did he want?"

"He asked me for the formula."

Emmett reared back. "You don't have it!"

"Of course not. I told him I didn't know what he was talking about."

"For the love of God!"

"What?"

"Thomas stopped the sale while the CIA took down the biologist." He pounded a fist into the opposite palm. "I should have put that together sooner. Isely must think your husband was somehow involved and left you the formula."

"He didn't. Trust me, I've been through everything. William would never have kept anything that sensitive. He'd have destroyed it first. I do remember him mentioning some big scientist who was off the market after a mission, but he never elaborated."

"That's it." Emmett shook his head. "Isely must have learned that loose connection and now he believes the formula is in your possession." Pacing now, he was clearly turning over the implications of this new information. He wasn't willingly shutting her out this time, but it was just as effective. "No wonder he pushed the idea of getting info on the director's family. That's what Isely wanted from the beginning. How did I miss this?"

Before Cecelia could think what to say, he wheeled on her. "Why the hell didn't you tell me this hours ago?"

"I knew you'd try to take me out of the equation." She stood, planted her hands on her hips. "That's all there is to discuss about that. Now, I'm going to take a shower," she said, falling back on a tried and true approach. Men talked more when their hands were busy. She hoped he was serious about the risks of leaving her alone and would join her rather than leave her here. "Then we should get breakfast."

Feeling his hot gaze following her, she unbuttoned his shirt as she walked toward the bathroom and let it fall at the doorway. She paused, giving him a tempting eyeful of her nude body before she stepped behind the door to start the shower.

She was under the hot spray, letting it beat at her scalp, convinced she'd made a tactical error, when the curtain went flying to the side. It required supreme effort to maintain her composure when faced with his sculpted body and obvious desire.

He was lean, but so well-defined an artist would never lack for inspiration. There was a balance to his form, an inherent strength that went far beyond the honed muscles.

She gave up the effort and licked her lips in anticipation. It saved her from smothering him with more flattery. Extending her hand, she would have testified sparks flew when he took it and joined her.

"Nice trick," he said, crowding her under the spray.

"I have more." She ran her hands up and over his chest.

"Prove it."

She proceeded to do just that.

Chapter Seventeen

Holt's legs were weak and he had the vague thought that he might embarrass himself and collapse in a satisfied heap right here in the dingy little bathtub.

She'd had tricks all right. Enough to surprise him, and he thought he'd seen it all. The woman was so much more than a first glance would suggest.

He had the absurd urge to ask if it had been like that with her husband. The question was taboo, and not at all the topic she wanted him to bring up, he felt certain.

Turning off the taps, he pushed the curtain aside and just enjoyed the view of her wrapped in a towel. This one was shorter than yesterday, and after what they'd shared, he figured ogling her was a compliment rather than overstepping.

"Like what you see?"

"You know I do." More than he should. They had a few more hours today, then it was over. He'd go his way and she'd go hers. It was for the best, but it put a sick feeling in his gut.

He pulled a towel off the rack and rubbed it across his hair, working his way down his body, pleased to catch her watching him, too.

Reluctantly, he put them back on task. "Isely approached me eight months ago in Monaco."

"Indebted gamblers make great marks."

He nodded, securing the towel at his waist. "Especially those of us with security clearances."

"No one on the outside knows about your team. How did Isely put it together?"

"I approached him. Or at least that's the way he made it seem. After what you told me I'm not so sure. I was on a mission to prove my worth to the great Thomas Casey."

Her pale eyebrows arched toward her hairline. "Well played either way. You wanted to get him and he needed something. Everyone lies and who wins?"

"Going on the offense is what I do. I lost brilliantly, on purpose, of course, then offered to sell him what I'd heard he was looking for."

"The agent who'd killed his father."

Holt nodded once more.

"He didn't bother to dig into your claims?"

"Of course he did. And I made sure he found what he needed to find."

"You lied." Her radiant smile made him want to confess the sordid details.

He reached into his bag for his razor and stopped. "Will it bug you if I don't shave?"

Her fingertips danced lightly along his jaw. "I like you a little scruffy."

He dipped his head for a kiss, needing another dose of her sweet taste. This one didn't burn as a prelude to seduction. No, it rocked him with something warmer, more real and far more dangerous to his sanity.

She dropped her towel across the edge of the tub and sauntered out to the bedroom to dress. He couldn't follow her and indulge in another sexual romp. They had to finish this thing.

He told himself this wasn't the woman to care about. She was so far out of his league, but damned if he didn't want to go for it anyway.

He was only a few minutes behind her, but when he emerged from the bathroom, she'd dressed and had her bag packed and her tablet in her lap. Her efficiency was disappointing.

"You're leaving the dress here?" It was still hanging in the closet.

"It's a bit bulky."

She was being practical. But he was going to miss it. "And it's something for your brother to find."

"He's not supposed to be looking."

"You can't believe he's just ignoring your disappearance."

"A girl can hope." She set the tablet aside. "Where is the meet?"

Holt tossed the towel to the side in favor of clothes more suitable for the day's events. He felt her eyes on him as he tugged on jeans and drew a shirt over his head. It seemed in one area at least—passion—they were well matched.

"I'll explain on the way."

"Tell me there's time to eat something."

"Jittery?"

She smiled, slow and wicked. "No. Just famished from so much exertion."

"There are a couple of meal bars in my bag."

"There has to be another choice."

He grinned when her stomach growled. "There's a decent diner a few blocks away."

"Great." She popped to her feet. "We can plan how to take him down. I have some ideas churning."

"Sure." He felt her staring as he packed up his computer. When he looked up, he realized his plan to keep her out of harm's way would never work. "Relax. I have some gear in the car. You can be my backup while Isely tries to sweat me for you."

She pumped her fist and turned a quick circle. "Good answer."

AN HOUR LATER, they'd demolished a hearty breakfast and finalized their plan. She'd used her tablet to review a few documents related to her husband's estate, but so far hadn't found anything about the formula Isely wanted.

That was good news from his perspective.

As he topped off her coffee, he realized he had to tell her the whole truth. Only an idiot would keep playing the role that would never come true. Call him an idiot.

He scrubbed at his face and tried to smile when she shot him a concerned look.

"You okay?"

"I'll be fine." Maybe the better play was to see how far they could get, to wait until he knew she loved him. Then maybe she'd be too attached to dump him and hold him accountable for all the lies.

Strange as it was, he couldn't imagine his life without her in it. Staying with her would only make the pain worse when she left him a week, a month or a decade from now.

And she would leave. Women like her didn't stay with men like him.

It boiled down to one critical question. Did he love her enough not to hurt her? The answer was obvious.

"Are you always nervous before a meet?"

"Nerves keep you on your toes," he said. "But this meet is the most important of my life."

"It will work out, Emmett."

"You've contacted your brother?"

"And his wife, just in case Thomas blows off my message."

"After this, he'll see what I've known all along. You and ops are a perfect fit." He laced his hand with hers. "He'll try to recruit you away."

"Not a chance."

If she went into ops, they'd never work together. He pulled himself away from that slippery slope. First he had to survive today, and then he had to convince her he could leave his past behind.

The past. He didn't want her to hear it from a third party and Isely would know she was close, would try to use it against him. She deserved better than that.

"About that New York job." The words stuck in his throat.

"The one that caught Thomas's attention?"

"Yeah." He swallowed, searching for the right words. He couldn't believe how much he wanted her to understand.

"Emmett, you don't have to tell me. I don't want you breaching security after everything else you've managed to protect during this sting operation."

"The things I've leaked, even to protect myself, are punishable offenses. But the one I regret, the one I should have found a way to tweak, is revealing the director's family. Revealing your existence to a monster."

"Thomas won't punish the hero who single-handedly stopped his nemesis and protected the secret of Mission Recovery. Besides, I think we both know now that getting to me was Isely's intent all along."

Hero? She was making this so tough. He knew Thomas wouldn't see him as a hero, even if things worked out the way she hoped. When she learned the truth, he'd be lucky if she could look at him at all. "Cecelia, just listen a minute. Isely knows things about my past. I'd rather you heard them from me first."

Even if she hated him for seducing her, for having the audacity to think he loved her, he knew she wouldn't abandon Thomas's cause. Whatever Isely said or did at this meet, she was strong enough to take over and finish what he'd started.

"When your brother found me, I was about to do a second stretch in prison for theft."

She didn't flinch at the news. Her calm blue gaze held his with a depth of compassion he didn't expect or deserve.

"Someone already told you. Who?"

"You." She covered his hands with hers. "Just now."

That was impossible. Maybe it was shock. "Did

you hear me? Did you understand what I meant?" He rubbed the back of her hand with his thumb. "I've served time for theft. I'm a thief and a liar. Take away the cool job and fancy office and I still am."

"Only because the mission required it. And even now you're still trying to prove yourself to my brother when you wouldn't be in the position you're in if he hadn't been convinced from the beginning."

"Cecelia, be reasonable here."

She reached up and those soft, pampered fingers caressed his cheek. "What were you expecting? I haven't had a temper tantrum since I was thirteen."

"Then have at it. You're long overdue." He stared out the window, not wanting to see the disappointment on her face when she accepted the truth.

"No, thanks."

"I'm sorry for—"

"For what?"

Her voice had a definite edge now. He met her gaze, leaned back a bit from the intensity.

"Don't you dare apologize for the past two days or the actions that brought us together."

"But—"

"I thought you were the one person who understood I don't scare easy. Was that a lie?"

"No, that was true."

"Well, here's some more truth for you. I'm a big girl and I know everyone comes with baggage. I don't care who you were or what you did. I love the man you turned yourself into."

She loved him? Had to be a figure of speech, although he supposed she would know more about it, having sustained a marriage from "I do" all the way to her husband's untimely death.

Maybe he wasn't just the short-term guy filling the holiday void for a society matron eager to explore a latent bad-boy fixation. He'd never been more frightened of what that might mean.

"I know we have to go our separate ways when this is over, but I wanted you to know where I came from."

"Please." She gave a little snort. "You wanted me to run away."

"No." *Maybe a little.*

"You're stuck with me, Emmett Holt, and I think you're warming up to the idea."

"You can't be serious."

"As a heart attack." Under the table, she rubbed her calf against his. "I wasn't raised to view people as disposable."

"Ops training will cure you of that," he said, checking his watch. He needed to get into position so Isely wouldn't have reason to suspect anything had changed.

"I doubt that."

"How can you be so sure?"

"I've learned a few things by watching you." She ticked the list of names on her fingers, "Casey, Thomas and William. Integrity and honor are honed—not dulled—by doing what's right and making the hard choices that protect others."

Holt wanted to believe her. With everything inside him, he wanted to believe in a pretty future where all the things she implied were possible. "You and I are worlds apart, Cecelia."

"But we don't have to be," she said softly.

"We should go." He tossed a few bills on the table to cover the check, then started scooting out of the booth. "Remember to chatter nonsense. It'll annoy whoever's listening on Isely's end, make them think you're flighty."

"One thing first."

He froze, hoping she'd give him another "I love you," another chance to say the words back.

"I have a secret, too."

Whatever it was couldn't be as bad as his. She was just trying to make him feel better, but he listened anyway. "Go on."

"I didn't cry when William died."

He didn't see the relevance, but he saw her lower lip tremble and knew there was more.

"I've never told anyone." Her breath stuttered,

then she gathered herself. "It happened about two months before he died. His last good day."

"That's when you cried."

Her chin jerked twice. "No more tears after that day. And I vowed never to care that much for another man again."

Talk about brutal honesty. He didn't know what to say, couldn't have said anything anyway. The vicious ache in his chest made it impossible. Now he knew why he lied, why he pushed people—women—away. Because love hurt.

And he was looking at a woman who'd loved and lost in a tragic fashion. She'd accepted his secret, he'd accept hers. "Understandable," he managed after a moment.

"Is it?"

"Yeah."

"I used to think so."

He wanted to pounce on that ray of hope, but they were out of time. "Come on. We have to go."

They walked to the car in silence, but as he reached to open her door, he changed his mind. He couldn't give her the words, but he could damn well show her how he felt, whether she could reciprocate or not. Maybe his emotion could help her rediscover her own.

He grabbed her close and kissed her, pouring out all the feelings he'd imprisoned inside.

Chapter Eighteen

Cecelia couldn't believe she'd told him her darkest secret. She was still reeling from the fierce kiss he'd planted on her in reply. It took everything she had to think up some inane chatter to irritate Isely's crew.

Emmett had located her at the perfect vantage point for watching the meet through binoculars. She wasn't happy about it, but she was here, overlooking his position at a small café. He'd told her it was to watch his back, but she knew it was another of those moves to protect her.

"Are you done with your shopping?" she asked, feigning excitement for the benefit of those listening in on their communications link.

"Never started."

"Did you make a list for Santa?" she teased, trying to pull him out of the shell he'd withdrawn into since the diner.

"No point. I'm always on the naughty list," he said.

Even through the earpiece, she caught the sensual undertone in that comment. After last night, she should expect her share of coal in the stocking, too. Thank goodness he couldn't see her blushing at the memory of how good they'd been. Together.

"Then what are your plans for Christmas?" She couldn't quite believe she was going to ask him to join her in the Caribbean. This probably wasn't an appropriate discussion under the circumstances, but she wasn't sure she'd get another chance to tell him what he meant to her.

"I don't make holiday plans."

"No family to visit?" She watched the slow shake of his head through the binoculars. "Not everyone is like you and yours."

"So that part of your profile was real?"

"Yes."

Hearing the edge in his voice, she knew his patience with the topic was about to snap.

"You should join me. I have a ticket—"

"This conversation could be monitored," he grumbled from behind his coffee cup.

"Yes, sir." Where was Isely? Had he gotten close enough to see that she wasn't with Emmett and walked away? Part of her couldn't help but hope... but then they might never get him and be able to clear Emmett's name.

"Why won't you be with family?" he asked, drawing her attention back to where it was supposed to be.

She sighed. "We've had enough togetherness for one season. I need a change of scenery."

"To get ready for your next phase."

She didn't like the implication behind that comment. He wasn't a phase to her. Although what else could he conclude after she'd said what she had about not loving anyone again?

"It's easier my way," he said. "No family. No plans. No problems. I'm spending the holiday on my boat."

"Sailing away into the sunset?" a male voice asked.

Cecelia jumped at the voice, even as she watched Isely sit down at the table with Emmett. "Sounds positively romantic. At least it will be when the women realize you are wealthy."

"Can't wait," Emmett said.

Isely looked at his jaw, still swollen from the fight in the hotel. "Did you run into something?"

"I tripped on a box of hammers."

"How unfortunate. Where is my new friend?" He glanced around. "She is supposed to be here, no?"

"Safe. I'm happy to make the introduction if you'll tell me when and where."

"Mr. Holt, it is a cold day. I would like to know

that my investments have not been in vain. I fear you are playing games with me now, and I have no patience for games, my friend."

"I've delivered everything you've asked for," Emmett ground out between clenched teeth.

Cecelia swore. If this conversation wound up in the wrong hands, it was just more evidence on the growing heap against him. It was as if he wanted every agent to swarm in and bury him for life. He was better than this, but the breadcrumbs he'd left would only help if someone cared enough to go looking. At this point, she was his last chance.

She couldn't make a mistake.

"And I have shown the agreed-upon appreciation," Isely said. "You have not cooperated with your new team. This is not a good sign."

"We had an understanding. I don't answer to your team."

Isely sighed. "You caused many injuries."

"You should have told me directly about a change in plans."

"I'm telling you now." Isely looked around the park once more. "I think you have developed an affection for the woman."

"She's business. You assured me you wouldn't harm her."

"And I will not. But you, I think, is another matter altogether."

Cecelia's lips tightened to prevent telling the

monster he wasn't harming a hair on Emmett's head while she still had breath.

"Then why bother with any of the rest of it?" Emmett demanded. "I've done all you ask. When guests from last night's gala start dying, you'll have won."

"That was for my own entertainment," the bastard said with a laugh. "Besides, I've heard no reports of this. Perhaps you've double-crossed me."

"What is it you want me to do, Isely?"

"Bring me the woman. She is useful in other ways. More useful than you."

Through the binoculars, Cecelia saw the other man approach, but her warning to Emmett came half a second too late. The man appeared to slap Emmett on the side of the neck. Emmett jerked. Was there something in his hand? Fear tightened around her heart. She watched the shock on his face and knew she was right. Tears welled in her eyes. She wanted to race to his side but he had made her swear she wouldn't move until he said the word.

Damn him! What was she supposed to do?

"Deliver her to this warehouse and you'll have the antidote in plenty of time to enjoy the wealth I showered upon you."

Antidote? Had he poisoned Emmett? Oh, dear God! She watched the monster tuck a card into Emmett's pocket.

"What did you give me?" Emmett demanded, his words slurred.

"Sometimes the old ways are better." Isely leaned close. "Don't worry. It is not contagious. Keep cooperating, Holt, and all will be well."

She watched in horror as Emmett's head lolled to the side. From this distance she couldn't shoot the bastard who'd done this. She couldn't reach him in time if she rushed toward them… She needed help.

Isely leaned over Emmett and his voice sounded in her ear. Cultured and slick, it made her want to take a shower. "Are you listening, Mrs. Manning? I do believe I might have given your lover too much. But perhaps he will survive until you get him to the warehouse for the antidote. The address is on the card in his pocket."

She wished she could put a bullet straight through his brain, to hell with his endgame.

Cecelia clenched her teeth and held her scathing reply as well as her position until Isely walked away. It required a measure of strength she didn't know she still possessed.

"Faster," she muttered, hoping she could hasten his departure by sheer force of will. If she bolted to Emmett's side too quickly, Isely would have them both in a snare.

She couldn't let that happen.

As soon as Isely and his cohort were long gone, Cecelia rushed to Emmett.

"Hang on," he mumbled, lurching to his feet. "I'm coming to you."

"I'm here," she assured him as she tucked herself under his sagging weight. "What did he give you?" She practically dragged him toward the car. It was hardly a block away and it felt like miles.

"I was hoping you'd know," he slurred. "...says there's an antidote."

"I heard. Let's go get it."

"No. He'll make me hurt you."

"Too late," she muttered.

"What?"

"I'm already hurt, Emmett." She turned her face up to his face. "Just because you're hurting."

"Forget about me. Call the authorities." His words were scarcely intelligible now. "You deserve better."

"You're right." She deserved a man who treated her as an equal. As he'd done from the start. A man who trusted her to watch his back while he tried to keep her safe from a criminal like Isely. She deserved a man who accepted his personal worth and shouldered her darkest secret. "When this is over and you're feeling better, we'll hammer out new terms."

He didn't say anything. He'd passed out.

Cecelia waved down a taxi and got him into the

back seat while explaining her friend had drunk too much. No way she could get him all the way to where they had parked the car. She dug the card from his pocket and checked the address, then provided it to the driver. She couldn't believe it had come down to this. Her against an international crime boss, the lives of two men she loved on the line.

Her whole body shook as she moved around to the other side of the car. She had to keep it together. Isely wanted Thomas to suffer. He had a flair for the dramatic, and based on what she'd learned from Emmett, he had impeccable timing. A dead man would have less impact on a man like her brother than a dying friend. This was just another part of the plan.

Isely would know that, would try to use that to rip Mission Recovery apart.

Well, he was in for a shock.

If Isely said the antidote was at the warehouse, that's where she had to go. And she'd arrive just as he expected: a weepy, worried mess. "Just like you taught me," she whispered to herself as she climbed in next to Emmett. "Give them what they need to see."

Her vision blurred and she realized she was crying. She swiped away tears, oddly relieved that she still had that depth of emotion inside her.

As she reached to close her door, a male voice interrupted. "Need a hand?"

She gave a startled cry when the square face of the burly security guard from the gala filled her window. "Go!" she shouted to the taxi driver.

"Wait." He flashed a badge. Real or fake, she didn't care at this point.

The taxi rushed away. She didn't have time to examine credentials or to verify a story. A plan was coming together in her mind. While it was dicey, it was hers, and she knew she could trust the players.

All she had to do was get word to them. Thomas would never question her need for help. He might not trust Emmett but he would do what needed to be done.

Failure wasn't an option.

She made the necessary call to Jo, Thomas's wife, instead of calling him. Jo promised to take care of everything. She said Thomas was already on it. Cecelia didn't know what that meant, but she was relieved to hear it. Thank God. She dragged a bottle of water from her bag and gave Emmett's shoulder a shove. "Come on, wake up."

His eyelids fluttered. "Where are we?"

"Doesn't matter. Drink this."

He shook his head. "No, thanks."

"Cooperate, Emmett." There wasn't much she could do without knowing the exact toxin in his system, but with something this fast acting, she knew his kidneys would need the help.

And who knew what dangers waited. She couldn't think about that or she'd freeze up. One step at a time.

Beside her Emmett muttered, but he kept sipping the water when prompted. Maybe Isely had done her a favor by incapacitating Emmett; now she wouldn't have to lie or hide what she was doing. In his condition he'd never remember her moves this afternoon—assuming they both survived Isely's final showdown.

She closed her eyes, thinking of the tropical paradise where she intended to spend Christmas day. They would all get through this.

Steadier, she called the marina and used her considerable influence as Mrs. Manning to arrange for Emmett's boat to be prepped, launched and moved around to the launch on the river.

A phone in his pocket rang and she knew the blocked number could only be Isely.

"Hello?"

"Ah, Mrs. Manning. It seems you've drifted off course."

"I—I know," she said, letting him hear her fear. Not of him or his petty plots, but that she might not be able to do what she knew it would take to eliminate him. "We had some car tr-trouble. The engine was acting funny. I had to get a cab. We're on our way."

"Now, now. I know this is overwhelming. Just bring him to me."

"We're on our way now. I swear."

"Good. Your brother is getting impatient."

"Thomas is with you?" Now she was panicked. Did Jo not know he'd been captured?

"What can I say? He insisted on crashing our party."

"Let me talk with him. Please?"

"Oh, we'll have plenty of time to chat in person when you arrive, Mrs. Manning."

The line went dead and Cecelia muttered a curse she'd learned from Emmett. The cab driver glanced at her in his rearview mirror. "Is everything all right?"

"Yes. Thank you." She shoved the burner phone deep into the seat cushion. It was only marginally better than tossing it out the window. No sense adding littering to the charges looming against Emmett. And her.

Beside her, Emmett's body shook with tremors.

Fear closed her throat. "Hang in there. It's almost over."

"Drop me off and go," he said, surprisingly coherent and with less slurring.

Was that good or bad?

"Absolutely not. I'm your backup."

"I can handle this."

"I believe you." No point arguing with a professional—particularly a man.

"Then let me do it alone."

"You'd like that, wouldn't you?" she argued. "Glory hound. I'm going in with you."

Emmett shifted, reaching for her face. She held his palm to her cheek when he didn't have the strength. This would not be their last moment. She refused to accept a future that didn't include him.

"Cecelia," he rasped. "Don't—"

"Shh," she interrupted, taking the water bottle. "Rest while you can."

His eyes drifted shut once more and Cecelia launched into a string of silent prayers. A few pleas for Emmett and Thomas mixed in, but what she begged for most was the courage to see this through.

Alexandria warehouse, 6:32 p.m.

HOLT WISHED HE'D been strong enough to shake off Cecelia when she'd refused to leave his side as they exited the cab at the warehouse. He wished he'd found a way to shield her from all of this.

Most of all he wished he'd told her he loved her when he'd had the chance. Falling in love hadn't been on the agenda for this op, but it had happened anyway. Ironic to come to terms with that now, when he was about to die.

His wrists burned where the cuffs bit into his skin, and the ache in his shoulders was too awful to contemplate. He'd been cuffed to a pipe above his head and the toe of his boot scraped the floor, but not enough to relieve the strain of his body weight.

Whatever Isely had given him was wearing off, but he didn't recall being dosed with an antidote.

"Wake up," a male voice hissed from nearby.

"Director Casey?" Holt tried to clear his dry throat. "That you?"

"Yeah."

"Cecelia?"

"I'm certain she's here…just not with us."

Holt's heart plummeted. What freakish use did Isely have planned for her? She didn't have what he was looking for. "Told her to go."

"Isely would have dragged her back. Whatever his endgame, she was part of it, I think before you were even involved. He's been plotting this revenge for years."

Holt wasn't so sure. She'd shown some interesting talents over the past days. Of all the things he'd done to protect Mission Recovery, he couldn't let the director believe he would have sacrificed Cecelia. "Never would've hurt her. You…must know…that."

"Shut up. Save your strength."

"What'd they give me?"

"A sedative, if it's what they gave me. Doesn't really matter. Keep breathing until we can find a way out of here."

"Never betrayed you." There were other things he should probably tell the director, but now wasn't exactly the time.

"You damn well blurred some lines," Thomas muttered.

If Thomas knew that, then he knew exactly what Holt had done. A glimmer of something close to hope flared in his chest. "If we get out of here, I'll get glasses," Holt joked despite the bleak circumstances.

"If we all get out of here, I'm going to beat the hell out of you and then I'll pat you on the back for getting that bastard."

"Anything." Anything but a resignation. He'd been ready to defect, to die if necessary to protect Thomas and Mission Recovery, until he'd met Cecelia. She made him want more than the solitary existence he'd been living long before going undercover to stop Isely. Two days with her and he believed in dreams again. With her.

Even if she couldn't feel as much as he did, he wanted her. Whatever she could give.

He peered up at his cuffed wrists. There had to be a way to get out of this.

A high-pitched cry ripped through the thin corrugated-metal walls, derailing his thoughts.

Holt jerked against his restraints even as Thomas ordered him to calm down.

"He's testing us."

"It's not her fight," Holt growled. He was done playing opossum. Drawing his knees up to his chest, he growled in frustration. There was no foothold he could find, no weakness he could exploit.

"Be still. You're going to need your strength when it'll actually do some good."

"Only when I'm dead."

The door opened and Holt squinted against the bright light. "You should listen to your boss," Isely said, stepping into the room.

Holt's vision was clear enough to see Thomas attached to a chair in the corner.

"Give it up. You won't get away with this," Holt warned.

"Just as I suspected." Isely stayed just out of reach of Holt's legs. "You were too weak to choose the right side."

"It's my underdog complex," he said through gritted teeth. "Let the woman go."

"But she is the whole reason we are here. Have you learned nothing through our talks?"

"Only that you're an—"

"Ah, yes. Vulgarity suits you well, Mr. Holt.

Much better than a tuxedo, or the fine lifestyle my payoffs would have funded."

"Might want to invest your money in a better chemist, Isely. That dose of poison seems to have worn off." He kept Isely distracted, hoping to give Thomas an opening. They had to get Cecelia out of here.

Isely revealed a Taser and Holt jerked with the force of the electricity coursing through his body. He should have seen that coming. But it'd be worth it when Thomas made his move. *Come on, man,* he urged silently. *I'm waiting for the big bad Thomas Casey to rescue me.*

"Aren't you the prince of deception?" Isely taunted. "Or is it thieves? It's no concern of mine. I only gave you enough sedative to cause panic and make the woman cooperate."

Holt swore. His instincts had warned him she'd been holding back, but just how much? What information could a CIA admin have that Isely needed?

"She cares for you," Isely said, zapping him again. "Pathetic, but I found it quite useful. I have everything I need now. Except the ending to this story."

"Enough," Thomas shouted.

They both knew that when Isely was done posturing he'd kill all three of them. Whatever he thought Cecelia had given him, it would never save them.

"Willing to talk at last, Director Casey?"

"Your father built his business and reputation on intelligence, not cruelty."

"You weren't his son," Isely said with a dreadful calm. "But your family will soon know the pain and bitterness of defeat."

"You've kidnapped three American citizens. You have to know that won't go unanswered."

"Really?" Isely crossed the room to tower over Thomas. "Who will act on your behalf? Who knows to ride to your rescue? Not your government. You don't even exist! Not your precious secret team. They think that one of you is a traitor and they don't yet realize you are gone!"

"I can tell you who really ruined that sale of the virus in Oberammergau," Thomas offered.

Isely jerked his chin toward Holt. "He has already told me."

Holt sensed defeat closing in around them. "I lied."

Isely crossed the room and shot him with the Taser again. "I know that! And by your omission, I have found the truth."

"If you let them walk out of here alive, I'll answer any question," Thomas offered with admirable calm.

Holt struggled to breathe. Thomas couldn't roll over like this. "Not for me," he challenged.

"Oh, is there honor among liars and thieves after all?" Isely's bitter laughter clanged against the metal walls of their prison. "Not in my experience. No matter. I have a better surprise. Load her up," he shouted.

The door opened and Thor pushed Cecelia, hands bound and feet chained, into the open doorway. "We're going far away now," Isely promised. "And there is nothing either of you can do except enjoy the ride."

Holt flexed and kicked, but Isely fired the Taser again. His mind drifted away from the pain and he blacked out with Thomas's fury and Cecelia's tears ringing in his ears.

Chapter Nineteen

The boat rocked gently under Cecelia as the yacht motored down the Potomac toward Chesapeake Bay. She was cuffed to a door in the engine room, and the sound and fumes were making her dizzy.

Isely crouched beside her, flipping through files on her tablet. Jo had come up with the plan. A Specialist, the burly man who'd tried to show her some ID before she got into that taxi, had located the car where Cecelia and Emmett had left their things. They had loaded the necessary notes and fake formulas on her tablet. Everything Cecelia needed to make Isely believe that her own husband had stolen the formula from the biologist he'd scarcely known other than on paper.

Cecelia prayed it would work long enough for help to get to them. As soon as she'd told Isely where the formula was, he'd sent two of his men to retrieve her tablet. Mission Recovery was watching the car. Hopefully backup was able to follow the goons here.

Isely was too smart to wait around for the tablet. He'd loaded them onboard his yacht and headed out to sea, hoping to reach international waters before he was intercepted. They were barely out of port when his goons had arrived with the tablet Cecelia had claimed was her husband's.

Now, if only Isely bought the credibility of the formula.

"I thank you, dear," Isely said as he studied the photos and diagrams. He gave a pleased nod and closed the device. He handed the tablet to one of his men. "Lock this in my estate room."

The man hurried to do his bidding. To the other man, he asked, "Is everything ready?"

A nod gave him the answer he wanted.

"Then we go." He unhooked Cecelia's cuffs and hauled her to her feet.

"You're a monster," she said as Isely pushed her up the narrow stairs toward the stern of the boat. "That formula should stay buried." Didn't take much to make her indignation sound real.

"So a few million people die. A vaccination will be discovered." The bastard shrugged. "This world is overdue for a cleansing."

She gasped when she saw Emmett and Thomas on their knees at the edge of the deck. Two more of Isely's crew stood behind them. Isely removed the chain at her feet and then her handcuffs.

"You can help with that effort, starting today."

"What?"

He handed her a gun and she immediately aimed it at him. "Good riddance."

"Now, now." He smiled at her. "You can't shoot me, my dear. My men will kill yours and then you. Everyone loses."

Her hands trembled. "Why are you doing this?"

"Because it needs to be done," he barked. "I've read the reports, spoken with the survivors. I know how my father suffered. Now your family will suffer."

"I gave you what you wanted," she cried, her heart pounding for real. Where the hell was backup? They had to be close.

"You're a woman. You weren't raised to know how men conduct their business. This is something you cannot possibly understand."

Her finger twitched on the trigger at the insult, but this wasn't about her. This was about inflicting lasting pain. Isely wanted her brother to suffer a loss as deep as he'd suffered. She and Emmett were merely a means to that end. It was obvious to her he intended to make this confrontation very personal and agonizing for Thomas, and then he would kill her anyway.

"Call off your men. Stop this nonsense."

"You lovely, sentimental woman." Isely threw back his head and laughed. "The time for begging has passed." In three quick strides he was beside her. "Remember our previous meeting. Have you made a final decision? Who survives? The clock is ticking, Mrs. Manning."

His taunting snapped her out of the red haze blurring her vision. She wasn't Mrs. Manning anymore. Those days were long gone. She was the woman who loved her brother with all her heart and Emmett Holt just as much.

"Come now. The final decision can't be that difficult. You only have to shoot one. Your brother or your lover?" He smiled patronizingly at her.

"Either way, you won't let me live."

"Not true. Someone must explain the mess to the authorities. It won't be me." His smile evaporated and all of his slick charm dissolved into so much cold hatred. "Someone must bear the consequences and someone must take the blame."

"I'll only tell the truth," she said, keeping her gun trained on Isely.

"Oh, but the truth is nothing more than smoke and fog without the right evidence."

And according to what Emmett had been feeding him, Isely believed the evidence condemned the man she loved, destroyed her brother's reputation and exposed the entire Mission Recovery team to what would surely be a media frenzy.

She looked at Emmett and knew what he wanted her to do: get out alive, with or without him. Worse, she knew what he expected her to do: walk away from his corpse.

Well, if the past forty-eight hours had taught her anything, it was the utter folly of expectations.

Two days ago his doubt in her fortitude might have stung her pride; now she understood the value of being underestimated, though they would damn sure have a long talk about the importance of sharing honest feelings when this was over.

"Choose, Mrs. Manning...."

Ignoring Isely's continued gloating, she looked to her brother and said a prayer that he could somehow give her a sign as to what she should do.

"Brother or lover," Isely prompted with that faint urbane European accent. "It is a difficult choice."

"Lia, you know what to do," Thomas said quietly.

She looked into his eyes for a long moment and she realized he was right. She did know what to do.

The boat rocked under her feet. Couldn't they have done this on land and increased her odds of success?

"Not a tough choice at all," she said to Isely, pulling the trigger as she spoke and firing at her brother. He toppled over.

In their shock, the remaining men gaped while

she sent another bullet into the knee of the man holding a gun on Emmett.

The man went down with a violent scream. The boat rocked and Cecelia stumbled backward, a stupid grin splitting her face as she watched Emmett launch himself at Isely.

Her brother quickly subdued and cuffed Isely's other lieutenant.

Cecelia took aim at the fight but couldn't get a clear shot, so she ran for the cockpit, holding the man at the controls at gunpoint until Thomas told her to do otherwise. With his help, they cuffed the man at the wheel and she reduced speed until they were idling.

"Sorry I shot you." She'd barely grazed his shoulder, but he'd toppled over before anyone realized she hadn't gotten him right in the heart.

"That's what you were supposed to do." He pulled her into a fast hug. "And you did good."

"Thomas!"

They both smiled at the familiar voice of Thomas's wife, Jo.

"I think that's my cue," Thomas said.

They both hurried to the deck. Specialists were securing all the bad guys. Jo was hugging Thomas. Cecelia searched through the crowd for Emmett.

"Are you injured, ma'am?" the man who'd tried to help her at the National Mall asked.

Cecelia shook her head, not trusting her voice,

trying her best not to burst into tears. It was over. It was really over. She looked around to see Emmett and Thomas talking quietly off to the side.

When the two men she loved most shook hands, she knew it was really over.

Chapter Twenty

Holt ached from head to toe, but nothing was sweeter than having Cecelia in his arms. He wanted to spin her around, but opted for pulling her into his lap while they motored back up the river. He couldn't deny that having Specialist Grant at the control of Isely's yacht gave him immense pleasure. The whole lot, Isely and his goons, were secured and under watch in the engine room.

"Your brother's going to punch me as soon as you're out of range. He's already warned me that he intended to beat the hell out of me. I think in all the excitement he just forgot. Or maybe being shot by his own sister has distracted him."

"Funny," she groused. "I think Thomas is too pleased with how things turned out to hold any grudges."

"Hope so." So far it seemed he still had a job. He tipped his head back and let the cool air wash over them for a moment. "You lied to me," he said, smiling with open admiration. "Thomas was already in place and backup was en route."

"I could lie to anyone," she replied. "I learned from the best. Besides, you were incapacitated."

"Hmm," he groaned.

"Hmm?"

"If you're so good at the lies, how will I know what's true?"

She walked her fingers up the torn front of his shirt, then fisted her hand in the fabric, pulling herself close for another hot, hard kiss.

"That is true," she said. "I never expected to love again, not like this. Thank you."

He tugged at her ponytail and gently tipped her head back so he could kiss the spot under her jaw that made her shiver. "I love you, too."

He smiled against her skin as her hands clutched at his shirt. "Say it again," she whispered.

He obliged, knew he always would where she was concerned. Her arms were chilled, so he hugged her closer. "You were magnificent today."

Her proud grin sliced right through his heart.

"Thanks. You did well yourself."

He shrugged. "CIA will be lucky to have you."

"If what happened here had actually 'happened'—" she used air quotes "—you'd be right."

"What're you saying?" He wasn't sure he could trust the hope that wanted to come to life.

"I'm looking at all of my options. Word is you're a hero. Got any pull at your place?"

"The boss might owe me a favor," he teased. He rubbed his nose against hers. "After he knocks me out. Still, I saved his sister."

She scoffed and pushed at his chest. "She saved herself."

"And me. You definitely saved me." He turned her in his arms and drew her back against his chest while they watched the shoreline of Alexandria approaching. "Is that my boat?" he asked as they neared the marina.

"I made a call," she said, "while you were fighting the sedative. We can cast off whenever you're ready."

"We?"

"If you'll have me."

She sounded nervous, but he didn't think it could possibly compare to the jitters he was fighting. He turned her around, made her look into his eyes so she would see the truth.

No matter what it cost him, he had to be completely truthful with her. "You're all I've ever wanted. My first and only Christmas wish. Say you'll marry me, Cecelia."

"Oh, yes! I will definitely marry you."

Before he could kiss her, they had moored the

yacht and were calling for everyone to report and clear the premises.

As he guided Cecelia off the vessel, Thomas Casey stopped him.

Before Holt could react, Thomas gave him a soft cuff to the jaw. "I don't know what you two have in mind for Christmas, but Jo and I would be happy to have you over for the holiday."

"I'm afraid we have plans," Cecelia piped up. "We're setting sail right now and wherever we end up on Christmas, we're going ashore and getting married."

Thomas frowned. Jo rushed up just then. "How romantic." She slugged her husband on the shoulder. "Isn't that romantic, honey?"

Thomas nodded and shrugged at the same time. "Absolutely. What about Casey?" He blinked, clearly startled.

"I'll send pics!" Cecelia wrapped her arm around Holt's. "We can all celebrate when we get back."

As they parted ways with the others, Holt drew her close and kissed her silky hair. "Is that really what you want to do? We can do this any way you want."

"This is perfect." She turned her face up to his. "I can't imagine celebrating Christmas any better way than saying 'I do' to the man I love."

He grinned. "Merry Christmas to me."

He kissed his bride to be, and less than an hour later they were making love on his boat with nothing but time and the sea in front of them.

* * * * *

LARGER-PRINT BOOKS!
GET 2 FREE LARGER-PRINT NOVELS PLUS
2 FREE GIFTS!

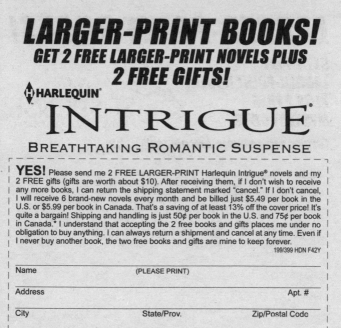

❦ HARLEQUIN®

INTRIGUE®

BREATHTAKING ROMANTIC SUSPENSE

YES! Please send me 2 FREE LARGER-PRINT Harlequin Intrigue® novels and my 2 FREE gifts (gifts are worth about $10). After receiving them, if I don't wish to receive any more books, I can return the shipping statement marked "cancel." If I don't cancel, I will receive 6 brand-new novels every month and be billed just $5.49 per book in the U.S. or $5.99 per book in Canada. That's a saving of at least 13% off the cover price! It's quite a bargain! Shipping and handling is just 50¢ per book in the U.S. and 75¢ per book in Canada.* I understand that accepting the 2 free books and gifts places me under no obligation to buy anything. I can always return a shipment and cancel at any time. Even if I never buy another book, the two free books and gifts are mine to keep forever.

199/399 HDN F42Y

Name	(PLEASE PRINT)	

Address		Apt. #

City	State/Prov.	Zip/Postal Code

Signature (if under 18, a parent or guardian must sign)

Mail to the **Harlequin® Reader Service:**
IN U.S.A.: P.O. Box 1867, Buffalo, NY 14240-1867
IN CANADA: P.O. Box 609, Fort Erie, Ontario L2A 5X3

Are you a subscriber to Harlequin Intrigue books
and want to receive the larger-print edition?
Call 1-800-873-8635 today or visit www.ReaderService.com.

* Terms and prices subject to change without notice. Prices do not include applicable taxes. Sales tax applicable in N.Y. Canadian residents will be charged applicable taxes. Offer not valid in Quebec. This offer is limited to one order per household. Not valid for current subscribers to Harlequin Intrigue Larger-Print books. All orders subject to credit approval. Credit or debit balances in a customer's account(s) may be offset by any other outstanding balance owed by or to the customer. Please allow 4 to 6 weeks for delivery. Offer available while quantities last.

Your Privacy—The Harlequin® Reader Service is committed to protecting your privacy. Our Privacy Policy is available online at www.ReaderService.com or upon request from the Harlequin Reader Service.

We make a portion of our mailing list available to reputable third parties that offer products we believe may interest you. If you prefer that we not exchange your name with third parties, or if you wish to clarify or modify your communication preferences, please visit us at www.ReaderService.com/consumerchoice or write to us at Harlequin Reader Service Preference Service, P.O. Box 9062, Buffalo, NY 14269. Include your complete name and address.

HILPI3R

LARGER-PRINT BOOKS!

GET 2 FREE LARGER-PRINT NOVELS PLUS 2 FREE MYSTERY GIFTS

Love Inspired®
SUSPENSE
RIVETING INSPIRATIONAL ROMANCE

Larger-print novels are now available...

YES! Please send me 2 FREE LARGER-PRINT Love Inspired® Suspense novels and my 2 FREE mystery gifts (gifts are worth about $10). After receiving them, if I don't wish to receive any more books, I can return the shipping statement marked "cancel." If I don't cancel, I will receive 4 brand-new novels every month and be billed just $5.24 per book in the U.S. or $5.74 per book in Canada. That's a savings of at least 23% off the cover price. It's quite a bargain! Shipping and handling is just 50¢ per book in the U.S. and 75¢ per book in Canada.* I understand that accepting the 2 free books and gifts places me under no obligation to buy anything. I can always return a shipment and cancel at any time. Even if I never buy another book, the two free books and gifts are mine to keep forever.

110/310 IDN F5CC

Name	(PLEASE PRINT)	

Address		Apt. #

City	State/Prov.	Zip/Postal Code

Signature (if under 18, a parent or guardian must sign)

Mail to the **Harlequin® Reader Service:**
IN U.S.A.: P.O. Box 1867, Buffalo, NY 14240-1867
IN CANADA: P.O. Box 609, Fort Erie, Ontario L2A 5X3

**Are you a current subscriber to Love Inspired Suspense books
and want to receive the larger-print edition?
Call 1-800-873-8635 or visit www.ReaderService.com.**

* Terms and prices subject to change without notice. Prices do not include applicable taxes. Sales tax applicable in N.Y. Canadian residents will be charged applicable taxes. Offer not valid in Quebec. This offer is limited to one order per household. Not valid for current subscribers to Love Inspired Suspense larger-print books. All orders subject to credit approval. Credit or debit balances in a customer's account(s) may be offset by any other outstanding balance owed by or to the customer. Please allow 4 to 6 weeks for delivery. Offer available while quantities last.

Your Privacy—The Harlequin® Reader Service is committed to protecting your privacy. Our Privacy Policy is available online at www.ReaderService.com or upon request from the Harlequin Reader Service.

We make a portion of our mailing list available to reputable third parties that offer products we believe may interest you. If you prefer that we not exchange your name with third parties, or if you wish to clarify or modify your communication preferences, please visit us at www.ReaderService.com/consumerschoice or write to us at Harlequin Reader Service Preference Service, P.O. Box 9062, Buffalo, NY 14269. Include your complete name and address.

LISLPDIR13R

Reader Service.com

Manage your account online!

- Review your order history
- Manage your payments
- Update your address

*We've designed
the Harlequin® Reader Service
website just for you.*

Enjoy all the features!

- Reader excerpts from any series
- Respond to mailings and
  special monthly offers
- Discover new series available to you
- Browse the Bonus Bucks catalog
- Share your feedback

Visit us at:
ReaderService.com

RS13